PUFFIN BOOKS

Carrie Hope Fletcher is an actress, singer and vlogger. Carrie has starred in a number of shows in London's West End and on national theatre tours, including *Les Misérables*, *The Addams Family*, *Heathers*, Andrew Lloyd Webber's *Cinderella* and more. She has written several bestselling books for adults and children.

Carrie lives just outside of London with Edgar the tuxedo cat and many fictional friends that she keeps on her bookshelves — just in case she ever gets lonely and wants the company.

THE DOUBLE TROUBLE SOCIETY

CARRIE HOPE FLETCHER

Illustrated by Davide Ortu

PUFFIN

PUFFIN BOOKS

UK | USA | Canada | Ireland | Australia
India | New Zealand | South Africa

Puffin Books is part of the Penguin Random House group of companies
whose addresses can be found at global.penguinrandomhouse.com.

www.penguin.co.uk
www.puffin.co.uk
www.ladybird.co.uk

First published 2022
001

Text copyright © Carrie Hope Fletcher, 2022
Illustrations copyright © Davide Ortu, 2022

The moral right of the author and illustrator have been asserted

Set in 13.3/18 pt Bembo Book MT Pro
Typeset by Jouve (UK), Milton Keynes
Printed and bound in Great Britain by Clays Ltd, Elcograf S.p.A.

The authorized representative in the EEA is Penguin Random House Ireland,
Morrison Chambers, 32 Nassau Street, Dublin D02 YH68

A CIP catalogue record for this book is available from the British Library

HARDBACK
ISBN: 978–0–241–55890–4

TRADE PAPERBACK
ISBN: 978–0–241–55891–1

All correspondence to:
Puffin Books, Penguin Random House Children's
One Embassy Gardens, 8 Viaduct Gardens, London SW11 7BW

This book is dedicated to all the kids with big imaginations.
Just because something is imaginary, it doesn't mean it isn't real.

Contents

1. Someone New in Town 1

2. Pancakes for Breakfast 19

3. Bad News 41

4. Poison 52

5. *Poisson* 59

6. Children Never Forget 68

7. The Circle is Broken 77

8. Inside Hokum House 92

9. Emerald and Amethyst 100

10. The Witch Returns 107

11. The Crows of Crowood 119

12. The Bond Between Friends 136

13. Taking Flight 144

14. Golden Words   156

15. Flying   163

16. Jemima Can Talk   174

17. No Room on the Broom   187

18. Good Luck, Amethyst   199

19. The Moon Appears   204

20. Stone   212

21. Two Sisters on a Broom   226

22. The Prophecy is Fulfilled   234

23. Time To Go Home   246

     Epilogue   257

1
Someone New in Town

They say that children born on Friday the 13th are immune to evil spirits. Both Ivy and Maggie had been born on exactly the same day of the same year under the same full moon, and both had been adopted by two single fathers who had recently moved to Crowood Peak.

The place was named as such because of its puzzling number of crows. The birds seemed to watch everything you did with an odd kind of intrigue, and they squawked back and forth to each other as if in conversation. They weren't bothersome exactly. Simply a little strange and creepy. It was named Crowood *Peak* because once upon a time there had been a small but proud mountain that loomed over the village that sat at its base. Most of the mountain was still there, but its peak was . . . well, nothing special these days.

Bill Eerie and Max Tomb had been great friends since they went to school together. They had called themselves the Double Trouble Society. (Well, exasperated teachers, fed up with their antics, actually gave them the name, but it stuck.)

The two fathers bestowed the name on their daughters, Maggie and Ivy, when they decided that they themselves were too old to get up to any further tricks, and it was clear that the girls had established the same unbreakable bond that their fathers had. For even as adults, Bill and Max were inseparable friends and had moved into houses so close to each other that only one house separated them.

It was a house that no one liked to talk about – some even called it *evil* – but Ivy and Maggie didn't worry about it too much; after all, they were immune to evil spirits, weren't they? But it didn't stop them checking for monsters under their bed each and every night . . .

The house between the two girls' houses was set away from the road, with a long path to the front door. Ivy and Maggie could look over its front garden and into one another's bedrooms through their side windows. It was much too far to shout, so their dads had given them a set of walkie-talkies when they were little, and they'd used them every night since. Mainly for their nightly monster hunt . . .

'Ivy for Maggie. Do you copy? Over,' Ivy whispered into her scuffed-up pink walkie-talkie. She sometimes wished they could forget the walkie-talkies and talk to each other on their phones, but she knew that Maggie would shrug at the idea and say: 'Where's the fun in that?' (It was something she often said!)

'Go ahead, Ivy,' came the reply. 'I copy loud and clear.'

Ivy's walkie-talkie crackled loudly and she quickly turned the volume down. It was only slightly past their bedtime and she didn't want her dad to cotton on to what they were doing – Bill Eerie was very scientifically minded and would laugh at the idea of monsters. Ivy also liked to think of herself as a rational, reasonable girl of science. She knew that monsters didn't *really* exist, but it didn't stop her being a little nervous when she looked under her bed. Well . . . quite a *lot* nervous, if she was being honest.

'We have a negative on the monster situation at this end,' Maggie added, using her best military voice. 'How's it looking over there? Over.'

Ivy scrambled to the end of her bed in the dark and swung the front half of her body over the edge. With her walkie-talkie in one hand, she slowly lifted the end of the duvet where it hung down. She took a deep breath and squeezed her eyes shut tight. 'Three . . . two . . .'

The crackle of her walkie-talkie sprang into life again and made her jump. 'What's taking you so long? Over,' Maggie whined.

'Don't rush me, Maggie! I have a process. Over.' Ivy took another deep breath, pushed her gold-rimmed glasses up her nose and squeezed her eyes shut again. 'Three . . . two . . .'

Her walkie-talkie fizzed. 'The longer you take, the more worried I am that there *is* a monster under your bed and it's eaten you! Over,' Maggie whispered.

'Shhh!' Ivy hissed.

'You didn't say "over". Over.'

Ivy could almost hear her friend smile through the line – there was nothing Maggie liked more than winding her up. She shook her head, took a deep breath and squeezed her eyes shut once more. *OK*, she thought. *Here we go.* 'Three . . . two . . .'

'JUST LOOK! *Over!*' Maggie shouted down the line.

Ivy rolled her eyes and knew if she didn't look now, she never would. She quickly ducked her head below the bed. She never expected to see anything other than her neatly lined-up shoes when she lifted the edge of the duvet, but she always worried about what would happen if she *did* become the very first person on Earth to discover a monster living under their bed. She'd be famous, of course – probably not as the first person to discover a monster, but as the first person to be *devoured* by one, pyjamas and all. So, when she finally opened her eyes and glared into the darkness and did, in fact, see two big green eyes glowing straight back at her, she felt shivers suddenly ripple over her skin, making her hair stand on end.

'Aargh!' she squealed, losing her grip and falling face first on to the floor, her walkie-talkie skittering out of reach.

'What's going on? I heard a big thump! Over!' called Maggie, her voice panicky.

Ivy reached for her walkie-talkie but it was too far away and she couldn't stop staring at the black shadow that was slowly moving towards her. Its eyes were fixed on her, and even though it looked like a small creature, she was certain that monsters had powers beyond her own imagination. It might be super strong and be able to throw her metres into the air, catch her in its jaws and swallow her whole, like those pythons that can eat entire sheep in one gulp! It might have laser vision and zap her into a pile of dust in a nanosecond. Or it might be able to wipe her memory, making her forget she ever saw it . . .

'Please don't eat me! Please don't eat me!' she whispered into the dark as the creature crept closer and closer. 'Please don't –'

'*Meeeeeooooowww!*' The black shadow jumped into the moonlight to reveal the pointed ears and whiskers of . . . a cat! But this was not any ordinary cat – it was the angry all-black cat that lived in the abandoned house next door. It often tried to scare Ivy and Maggie as they walked past every morning by hissing at them from the overgrown shrubbery or snagging their school jumpers with its claws. This was *not* the first time Ivy had found the cat in her room, and each time it gave her the heebie-jeebies.

'Ramshackle!' she said crossly, her shoulders slumping. Ramshackle sneaked out from under the bed and strutted over to the door, meowing, a purple gem on its collar shimmering in the moonlight. Then it turned to hiss at Ivy. Ivy dusted off her neat pink-and-purple-striped pyjamas and ran over to the door, quickly opening it so the cat could get out. Then she grabbed her walkie-talkie again, raced over to the window and pulled it up.

Maggie, in blue-striped pyjamas, was at her window, holding her green walkie-talkie. 'Was that stupid cat in your room again? Over.'

Ivy waved her walkie-talkie back, then they both watched Ramshackle, having left Ivy's house the same way it got in, sneak into the garden of the house between theirs and disappear into the tangle of overgrown greenery. Several crows cawed and fled from the foliage in a furious flap of wings.

Like the rest of the villagers, Maggie and Ivy mostly ignored the house between theirs. *Hokum House*, people called it. In fact, the house was part of the centuries-old legend of the Crowood Witch, and when the village held its Festival for the Twelve every blue moon, Ivy and Maggie had to fight through crowds simply to get to their own front doors, as so many people came to see it. They would lay flowers and candles in a ring round the house, to remember those who had been taken by the witch.

It wasn't a particularly happy story, and it certainly didn't have a happy ending, but the people of Crowood Peak enjoyed keeping this important piece of local history alive. Maggie loved the festival – she couldn't get enough of the legend – but Ivy just liked the decorations people made for the occasion. The next festival was coming up, and she was looking forward to it.

The house was so covered in moss, vines and birds' nests that it barely resembled a house any more. You could sort of see the windows if you got close enough, but only the bravest kids ever got that close. Even around festival time, Ivy and Maggie tried not to talk about the Crowood Witch, who supposedly used to live there. Ivy didn't want to talk about the witch because she didn't believe in witches, and Maggie didn't want to talk about the witch because she *did* believe in witches – and was really quite scared of them!

So it was quite a shock when Maggie suddenly did mention witches.

'Can you see that?' she asked in a whisper. A few crows had landed on the old broken fence in front of Hokum House. They cocked their heads to one side and peered up the street in the same direction Maggie was now looking.

'You didn't say "over". Over,' Ivy said teasingly.

'Ivy, I'm . . . I'm serious.' Even though Maggie was far away and Ivy couldn't see her expression, she could tell by Maggie's voice that something was up. 'Someone's approaching the gate.'

Maggie was looking up the street, past Ivy's house, so Ivy couldn't see what she was looking at yet. But she could hear a faint clip-clopping of heeled boots against the pavement, which got louder and louder as a figure in a hooded cloak walked into view. The hood came to a curiously long point that zigzagged down the person's back. Their face was covered mostly by fabric, but in the light of the moon Ivy could just make out lips painted the colour of ripe plums. This mysterious figure had a book held open in one black-gloved hand and a large black leather bag in the other.

'She looks like a . . . a . . .' Maggie gulped hard. 'A witch.'

'Don't even say it, Maggie. There's no such thing as witches,' Ivy said quietly. 'Besides, I doubt she'll be able to get much further. That gate has been rusted shut for forever; she won't have much luck opening . . . it . . .'

Ivy stopped talking as the cloaked figure waved their hand over the latch on the gate and read something out loud from the book they were holding – though Ivy and Maggie couldn't make out what was being said – and then the gate did the most peculiar thing. It trembled under the figure's fingertips and, as it shuddered, shed its rust. The crows cawed and scattered as all the flakes of peeling paint that had fluttered away in the wind now came back on the breeze and re-attached themselves to the gate, until it looked as good as new. When it was a glossy black colour once again it swung open without so much as a creak.

The figure closed the book and gave a single nod, satisfied with their work. But the weird goings-on didn't stop there. As the person walked up the long pathway, passing the girls' windows, every piece of each cracked paving stone rearranged itself like a puzzle, the cracks glowing bright white and then disappearing altogether, until the broken pathway was no longer broken. Each stone mended itself in this fashion before the person's boots made contact, so they had a perfect path to the door of Hokum House.

The person flicked through the book once again, and then Ivy and Maggie could both hear more muttering – although it sounded like gibberish – and the cloaked figure began to wave one hand high above their head. With a flick of the wrist, another even more peculiar thing began to happen. Bit by bit the house began to repair itself. Weeds and vines started to shrink away from the brickwork; shattered windows became whole and sparkling clean; the bats fled as the roof fixed itself; and the front door swung open with a satisfying thunk of the lock. It was as if a hundred invisible people were mending the house, except Ivy and Maggie couldn't see a soul.

Finally, the visitor set down their leather bag, slid the book inside and then reached up and removed the hood of their cloak. Ivy and Maggie both gasped as a cascade of bright blonde hair tumbled down a woman's back. Her skin was whiter than the moon that hung above the house, and seemed to glow in the same celestial way as she turned her face towards it and closed her eyes. She stood there for a moment, basking in the light as if she could feel its warmth, just like Ivy and Maggie could feel the heat of the sun on a summer's day.

Ivy was so enraptured watching this stranger she didn't notice her walkie-talkie slowly slip out of her hand until it was too late. It clattered to her bedroom floor and broke the silence of the calm night. The woman's eyes snapped open and up to Ivy's bedroom window. Ivy ducked down quickly, but not before seeing that the woman's eyes were a bright luminescent purple, which cut through the dark like a blade of amethyst.

'Ivy, come in! I repeat, Ivy, come in.'

Ivy scrambled towards the voice coming from her walkie-talkie, which had slipped under her bed. 'I'm here! I'm here!' she replied through jagged breaths. She pulled herself back up and peeked through the window again just as she heard the bang of a door closing and the click of a lock turning. The woman had disappeared inside the house – which now looked brand spanking new, as if it had been built only yesterday.

'So . . . it looks like we've got a new neighbour, then,' Maggie said. They stared at each other over the front garden of Hokum House in total disbelief at what they had just witnessed.

'She seems . . . spooky. She must be some sort of magician. Or . . . or a really fast house renovator,' Ivy said uncertainly, but she could feel Maggie judging her from across the way. Ivy refused to believe the alternative. 'I'm sure she'll make a lovely neighbour.' She squinted to see if she could see into the house and catch sight of the woman's eyes again. *They couldn't really have been purple, could they?* she thought.

'Ivy,' Maggie said, sighing.

'What?'

'*Iiiiivvvvy*,' Maggie said again, as if Ivy was missing something quite vital. Ivy was very good at examining facts, so it bothered her when she felt like she'd overlooked something important.

'*Whhhhaaatttt?*'

'She's so *obviously* a witch!' Maggie hissed through the walkie-talkie so violently that it came out at Ivy's end with a fizz. 'And does it suddenly smell weird to you?' Ivy could hear Maggie sniffing. 'Smells like . . . fruit. Like someone's just taken a cherry pie out of the oven.'

'I'm sorry, I think there's something wrong with our devices because it sounded like you said that the woman we saw go into Hokum House is a *witch*,' Ivy said, laughing, but only gently, as what they'd seen that woman do really had been impossible. 'And I can't smell anything,' she lied, even though her stomach was rumbling at the sweet and delicious scent filling the air.

'I said she was a witch the moment I laid eyes on her!' Maggie insisted.

'I know, but I thought you were joking! I thought you were talking about the way she was dressed! You know, that cloak with the hood . . . I didn't think you were genuinely suggesting she was capable of doing actual magic.'

'OK. First of all, Dad says never comment on other people's appearances, because it's none of my beeswax, and you know I would *never*!' Maggie said, scandalized. 'But *come on*, Ivy! We both saw her do a *whole house makeover* in less than a minute! When Dad had the kitchen redone, it took about three months!'

'Well, that was down to him changing his mind about the colour scheme thirteen times,' Ivy said huffily. 'Maggie, there is *no such thing* as witches. I refuse to believe it! It's very dark outside and it's really quite late, so I expect we're both tired, and someone moving in next door – that old house that has always been empty – has been quite a shock. I don't know what we saw, but it definitely wasn't *magic*.' Ivy yawned to emphasize exactly how tired she was.

'OK . . . but how about just for fun we –' Maggie began, but Ivy cut her off abruptly.

'Do not say what you're about to say.'

'What do you mean?' Maggie said, outraged.

'Please, Maggie. Whenever you say "but how about just for fun" it always ends up with us doing something that could get us killed, or *in double trouble*, and definitely *not* fun! So please don't say it . . . please, please, please . . .'

'But how about just for fun,' Maggie said excitedly, 'we go next door and pay our new neighbour a visit?'

Ivy was silent for a moment – Maggie's suggestion seemed totally absurd. Brave too, as she knew Maggie was scared of witches. But she also knew that Maggie would never let her fear get in the way of a good adventure. 'I am *not* knocking on that door,' she said at last, as if it were the final word in the conversation, although she knew it wouldn't be. With Maggie it never was.

'Why not? If she's not a witch, like you said she isn't, then that means she's an ordinary person and an ordinary neighbour.' Maggie had a sing-song tone to her voice; a tone Ivy had heard before when Maggie was trying to get something she wanted from her dad.

'But . . . but . . .' Ivy was struggling to find another reason not to go anywhere near that house.

'And *good* neighbours,' Maggie continued, knowing Ivy was trying to come up with an excuse, 'do nice things when someone new moves in. We could take her some flowers or a box of chocolates or something. We could make her a card and get everyone on the street to sign it.' Maggie knew that

Ivy was a stickler for good manners and that this idea would appeal to her.

'Fine.' Ivy sighed. 'But if she turns us into toads, I'll never speak to you again!'

'You'll never *croak* to me again, you mean?' Maggie said, laughing, but Ivy did not find it in the least bit funny. 'Besides, I thought you said there's no such thing as witches?' Ivy could almost see Maggie's mouth twisting into a wry smile from across the gap between their houses, her eyes twinkling mischievously in the moonlight. It seemed as though the possibility of a real witch had made her feel excited rather than scared.

The sound of a window scraping open startled them both. They ducked down a bit, peering over their windowsills to see where the noise had come from. One of the windows at the front of Hokum House was open and warm yellow light was pouring out on to what was now freshly cut grass. The woman with the long blonde hair and bright purple eyes poked her head out and made sucking noises with her lips. Sort of like the kind of noise you'd make to summon a –

'*Meeeeoooow!*' Ramshackle appeared from under one of the perfectly neat hedges that now lined the front garden. The cat jumped over the window ledge and disappeared into the house, and the woman closed the window again and drew the curtains. Curtains! The house actually had curtains now.

'How did she know about Ramshackle? That cat has been living in that house since before we were born, according to my dad,' Ivy whispered into her walkie-talkie.

'Didn't the Crowood Witch have a cat?' Maggie said, her voice quivering, hinting at how nervous she really felt.

'Maggie,' Ivy said, rolling her eyes.

'What?'

'*Maaaaagggiieee*,' Ivy said again, as if Maggie had suggested something outlandish. Maggie knew she had a vivid imagination, but what she thought was usually far more interesting and fun than the truth, so it bothered her when she was made to think logically.

'*Whhhaaaaat?*'

'Are you genuinely suggesting that a witch from a story that's almost three hundred years old has returned from the dead and has moved in next door? And that her cat has also survived three hundred years and they've now been reunited?' Ivy almost laughed as she said it.

'Stranger things have happened!'

'Like what?' Ivy scoffed.

There was a long pause on Maggie's end of the line. Then, 'All right, this would be the strangest thing to have ever happened in this boring place, but the legend does say that the witch will return!'

'D-d-does it?' Ivy said hesitantly, and Maggie gasped in shock.

'Haven't you read the legend of the Crowood Witch? It's what our village is famous for. There's the festival every blue moon – we've both been to more than one! And there's a blue moon coming up in a few days, so it's about to happen again.'

Ivy liked knowing about blue moons. Not everyone did. Her dad had explained to her how it only happened when there were *thirteen* full moons in a year. Usually, there were only twelve, three for each season. If there *were* four in one season, then the blue moon was the third of those four. That was why the festival didn't happen every year.

'All right, all right,' she said, guessing that Maggie didn't want a science lesson right now. 'I know the basic story, but I guess I never really took it that seriously. It's like a tale about Robin Hood or King Arthur. Those are old British legends, but you don't expect either of them to suddenly turn up and move in next door!'

'But the Crowood Witch isn't from just anywhere – she's from here! *Right here!* This very spot. And for your information, the Crowood Witch isn't just a story – it's a *legend*, and legends aren't made up!' Maggie cried.

'Legends are called legends because they *might* be true, but they happened so long ago that no one can be sure,' Ivy corrected her.

'Well, how about *we* find out if it's true or not? How about we kick-start this adventure by going to the library after school tomorrow and reading the original legend of the Crowood Witch?' Maggie suggested. 'You know Mrs Moody keeps it in a glass case. Then we can talk about taking our new neighbour some cakes to welcome her to the village. *If* she's not a witch. Although I'm sure by then you'll be totally convinced that twitchy-fingers next door is a witch, so you'll be way too scared to knock on her door.'

'I'm scared to knock on her door now, when I think she's simply a normal human woman who happens to be very handy at DIY!'

Maggie sighed and, for a moment, Ivy felt bad. Maggie was far more adventurous than she was, and Ivy did often have to step in and stop her from carrying out her grand plans. Usually because they were so dangerous – like the time Maggie went to the top of Crowood Peak to whizz down it on her roller skates in an attempt to break the sound barrier! But this adventure was only knocking on someone's front door to welcome them to the village. How dangerous could that be?

'Come on,' Maggie said, giving Ivy one last nudge. 'Where's your sense of adventure?'

'I think we both know I've never had one of those,' Ivy mumbled.

'Besides,' Maggie said, 'you know I'm going to go with or without you. Wouldn't you rather come with me to make sure I don't get myself killed or in trouble?'

17

Finally, Ivy sighed. 'One day, Maggie, you really are going to get us eaten by something or other, and when that day comes, I'm never going to speak to you again.'

'Love you too, Ivy! See you tomorrow for our best adventure yet!'

As they pulled their curtains for the night and climbed into bed, the chimney of Hokum House began to smoke . . .

2
Pancakes for Breakfast

Ivy woke the next day in the usual way, her walkie-talkie buzzing into life, with Maggie's voice coming through loud and clear.

'GOOOOOOOD MOOOOOORRRRNIIIIIINGGGG!' Maggie enjoyed singing so much that she made sure to make up a song each morning, especially for Ivy. '*Double Trouble is the name of our gang; Double Trouble is the song that I sang!*'

'That doesn't even make sense, Maggie,' Ivy said, yawning.

'Yeah, but it rhymes. Give me credit for trying. And shhh – I'm not done yet!' Maggie cleared her throat dramatically.

'Apologies. Please continue.'

'*Today is the day that we catch ourselves a witch! We'll tie her up with rope, then throw her in a DIIIIITCH!*'

Ivy leaped out of bed and ran to the window just in time to see Maggie pirouette and finish with jazz hands. Ivy laughed and gave her best friend a round of applause. Even when other slightly more worrying things were on Ivy's mind, Maggie was able to make her forget about them for a moment and giggle. However, now that she was at the window, Ivy couldn't help but inspect Hokum House. She would have thought it had been a very strange dream if it wasn't for the picture-perfect house that now sat next door, its chimney gently smoking. The woman in the cloak was nowhere to be seen.

'Still miraculously fixed, then?' Maggie said, leaning out of her window to get a better look.

'Seems like it. I'm gonna go and quiz my dad. See if he knows anything about that weird woman. Meet you in half an hour for school?'

'See you soon for the best adventure yet!' Maggie yelled.

'You know, the more you say that, the more I feel like I need to vomit,' Ivy said, sighing, as she went to get herself ready for the day ahead. She took one last look out of the window.

At first she thought it was her imagination – it was just a little thin plume beginning to form – but then it became more obvious and Ivy could see that the smoke coming out of the brick chimney was *sparkling*. It was as if purple glitter had been thrown into the fire and was getting caught up in the small tornado of smoke spiralling towards the sky. How peculiar . . .

Ramshackle was nowhere to be seen. Usually, the cat sat on the fence, swatting its paw at passers-by or angling the purple gem on its collar into the sunlight to shine in people's eyes as they walked past. Maggie always said the cat was doing it on purpose, but Ivy's dad told her not to be silly, that Ramshackle was an innocent, if slightly angry, moggy, and Maggie was only exercising her vivid imagination. However, despite being unsure whether cats had the ability to bully humans or not, Ivy was inclined to agree with Maggie. That cat always seemed to know exactly what it was doing.

'Have you seen the woman who moved in next door last night, Dad?' Ivy asked as she munched her cereal. She hadn't complained about the cereal, but it was quite unusual that her dad, Bill, hadn't cooked a proper hot meal. 'Breakfast is the most important meal of the day!' he always said. Bill would make breakfast each morning and then head to his shop in the high street. He helped people fix things when they broke – like computers, hoovers and toasters – but really he was an inventor. His best invention was a hat that detected the first drops of rain and immediately sprouted an umbrella out of the top, so you could stay dry and still have your hands free to do important things like carry shopping bags or hold the dog's lead. Ivy thought her dad was a genius, but the rest of the world wasn't so convinced – the umbrella-hat hadn't been snapped up by any manufacturer yet.

This morning, though, she had come downstairs to find her father having only a cup of coffee for breakfast, so she had rifled through the cupboards and come across an old box of cereal (it tasted rather like cardboard). The kitchen window was open and the smell of the smoke from next door had begun to seep into the kitchen. She had expected it to smell like burning wood – like the fires on Bonfire Night – but instead it smelled *sweet*, like burnt sugar.

'Dad,' she said, 'can you smell that fire from next door?'

'Next door? That's such a beautiful house,' Bill said, sighing longingly as he put down the latest copy of *Inventors' Weekly* and sipped his coffee.

'The house next door? *That* house?' Ivy said in shock, pointing out of the window to the house that before last night had been an absolute wreck. Her father was usually so quick to pick up on things – Ivy always said his brain raced at a million miles an hour – so it seemed bizarre that he hadn't noticed how quickly the house had become so picturesque. This was not like him at all. 'You mean Hokum House?' she questioned. 'It was a total mess, Dad!'

'I think you're mistaken, Ivy. That house has always been beautiful – I'm not sure why I never noticed it when I was looking to move here. I would have snapped it up instead of this place, but never mind! You live and you learn!' He laughed a hearty laugh that Ivy was sure she'd never heard before. It was like someone else's words and expressions were coming out in her father's voice. He looked and sounded like her dad, but it was almost as if something else was in control of what he was saying . . .

'Dad,' she said, a little worried but also frustrated, 'before last night, that house was run-down and falling apart. There were bats and mice and birds living in it! But this woman turned up last night and . . . and . . . now it looks like *that*!' She pointed even more animatedly out of the window.

Her father looked at her for a moment, his face blank and emotionless. But then it sank into a calm smile. 'Ivy, dear, how much sugar is in that cereal you're eating? I think maybe it's time we switch to porridge or fruit for a little while.' He closed his magazine and moved to the sink to wash up his mug, leaving Ivy to stare at him, completely puzzled.

Meanwhile, two houses away, Maggie was also feeling confused. She was yawning sleepily as she came down for breakfast, but came to an abrupt stop on the bottom step as the sweet smell of pancakes shot up her nostrils. As she breathed deeper, she realized she could also smell bacon, which she could hear sizzling away in a pan.

'Dad?' Maggie rubbed her eyes, not quite believing what she was seeing. Her father, Max, *never* cooked a hot meal in the morning. Breakfast in their house came in boxes or packets, or was simple, like jam on toast, because more often than not they both got up late and ended up rushing around to make sure they were on time for work or school. Dinner time was when her father excelled. He had a million cookbooks for extraordinary dinners, but breakfast? Maggie could only dream of bacon sandwiches, scrambled eggs and French toast. Today, however, was different. There was her dad, frying pan in hand, attempting to flip pancakes. At his feet was Frankenstein, their dog, happily eating the remnants of failed attempts from the kitchen floor.

'Oh, hello there, pumpkin! There's freshly squeezed orange juice on the table, and I'm almost done with the pancakes. Although it looks like we might only have one each. I had a bit of an accident with a few of the others – but at least Frank is impressed.'

Maggie grabbed a wooden spoon from the countertop, which was covered in pancake batter, and brandished it towards her father. 'Who are you and what have you done with my dad?' she said, half joking, but secretly wondering if he had in fact been replaced by a clone or a robot.

'Maggie! You're getting batter on the floor and Frank has already had more than enough. Sit down, silly.' He threw a sloppy, batter-covered tea towel over his shoulder and began to dish up.

'I'm serious. What's all this about?' Maggie asked as she took her seat at the table.

'I'm only making breakfast, Maggie!' her father replied.

'You've never made breakfast like this before,' she mumbled through a mouthful of burnt toast, taken from the pile her dad had put in the toast rack in the centre of the table.

'Well, there's a first time for everything!' Max sang, in a tone that sounded so unlike her father it sent a shiver down Maggie's spine.

'Speaking of things that are happening out of the blue . . .' Maggie said, eyeing Hokum House out of the kitchen window, 'the house next door! I mean . . . what happened there, eh?' she said, expecting him to understand exactly what she meant, but he furrowed his brow at her.

'What about it?' her dad asked.

'Well, look at it!' Maggie laughed, as if her father was the one being silly. Observation certainly wasn't his strong point, but this was a great big whopping change that no one could have missed.

Max leaned over and took a long look at the house, but then he simply shrugged, saying, 'Looks like it always does,' and he went back to trying to dislodge the pancake from the bottom of the pan.

Maggie's smile vanished instantly. 'Dad, are you trying to be funny? Because it's not working.'

'Hey, I'm always funny!' He nudged her as he set down a plate on the table. A solitary pancake sat sadly in the middle. It was burnt on one side, yet undercooked and almost runny on the other. Maggie pushed the plate away. She had lost her appetite.

'What? Dad! The house next door it's . . . gorgeous!'

'I know. I wish our house looked like that,' he said, sipping his tea.

'But yesterday it wasn't,' Maggie said firmly.

'Wasn't what, pumpkin?' Her father picked up his pen and went back to scribbling something down in his notebook. He was often scrawling illegible ideas for new stories at breakfast, but this time he seemed particularly feverish about it.

'It wasn't *gorgeous*! It was a rotten mess! It was an absolute dump, Dad!' Maggie put a hand gently on her father's writing hand so he was forced to stop and look directly at her. She needed him to see that she was serious. His brown eyes looked into hers but there was something off. He was looking at her, for sure, but he didn't seem to be *seeing* her.

'Is this another one of your stories?' he asked her. 'Are you writing one about Hokum House? Oh, I bet the *Crowood Chronicle* would love to publish something like that in the arts section for the coming festival. I'll pitch that to the team today, if you fancy?'

Her father worked for the local newspaper, in the creative-writing section. He wrote a story for them every week and had gained a little fame in their village. Max was always trying to encourage Maggie to follow in his footsteps, and ordinarily she loved that. They might not be biologically

related, but there was no denying she was Max's daughter –
storytelling was one of her favourite things in the world, and
if anyone was going to believe her story about the woman in
the house and the Crowood Witch, it was her father. Which
is why it was so odd and so frustrating that he couldn't seem
to understand what she was on about.

'No, Dad, it's not a story. Yesterday that house was almost
falling down. It always has been, ever since I can remember.
But today it's the most beautiful house ever, and there's a
woman living there with that awful cat.'

'A woman? Oh, you mean Amy,' Max said, munching on
his similarly pale yet crispy pancake.

'Amy?' Maggie screwed up her face in confusion. 'Who on
earth is Amy?'

'Amy, who lives next door? She's lived there for years,
pumpkin. You know that! Now, eat your pancake and get
yourself ready or you'll be late meeting Ivy for school.' With
that, Max promptly disappeared back into his notebook.

Maggie stared at her father in total disbelief. All remaining
traces of hunger gone, she left her soggy pancake on the plate
and wandered upstairs to get dressed. She certainly had a lot
to tell Ivy on their way to school.

'Your dad didn't believe you, either?' Maggie asked in shock
as they walked side by side, their matching backpacks, heaving
with books, threatening to topple them over backwards with

27

every step. Ivy shook her head at the pavement. While Maggie's dad was very much into fiction, Ivy's dad was into facts, so Maggie had been sort of counting on Bill Eerie to be the responsible adult and figure out what was going on. However, Ivy had been counting on Max Tomb to believe it, seeing as he was so good at writing stories.

Ivy and Maggie had been let down on both counts.

'My dad insisted the house had always been like that,' Ivy said, sighing.

'My dad insisted that the woman we saw has lived there for years. He even said her name was *Amy*.'

'*Amy?* She definitely didn't look like an Amy. She looked more like a . . . a Morgana or a Bellatrix.'

'Yeah, Amy does seem a bit tame for someone who might have magical powers that could potentially wipe out our entire village and life as we know it . . .' Maggie said.

Ivy stopped dead in her tracks and turned as pale as the underside of Maggie's breakfast pancake. 'What?!' she gulped.

'Oh, Ivy. You need to read the legend.'

For Maggie, school seemed to drag on and on. Her legs bounced up and down under her desk in anticipation. Even when they were reading her favourite book in English she couldn't concentrate on the words on the page because she kept thinking of bits of the legend of Crowood Peak – words she had read time and time again. She couldn't wait to show the original to her best friend. It was only when Isaac Hedges nudged her, sloshing his beloved jar of frogspawn, that she realized it was her turn to read aloud. Isaac was a gentle boy with a deep love of nature. He was often found by the school pond making friends with the toads, and the clean uniform he arrived in would always be covered with mud and pond slime by the time he got home.

'Sorry, miss . . . what page are we on?' Maggie asked sheepishly, looking down quickly at the same time to check no frogspawn had landed on her skirt.

For Ivy, however, the day was moving far too quickly for her liking. She was so preoccupied watching the minute hand of the clock speedily slice its way through the hours that she accidentally mixed the wrong chemicals in her chemistry lesson. She didn't notice until Eddie, her science lab partner and the only person in school whose grades rivalled her own, grabbed the fizzing test tube from her hands, quickly put it in its holder and dragged her by the scruff of her lab coat under the desk. There was a dull *FWOMP* noise, quickly followed by the sound of shattering glass and a shriek from a few other students. When they peeked over the edge of the desk, the test tube was in a hundred tiny pieces and a strange green liquid was soaking into their exercise books.

Even so, Ivy's main concern wasn't the fact that she now had a note from her chemistry teacher to give to her father, it was that she was even closer to reading the legend with Maggie. She knew it would probably give her nightmares, or keep her up that night worrying about the woman who lived next door and whether she really could wipe out their village.

Ivy knew bits and pieces from the legend, of course. The festival they held to commemorate the vanquishing of the Crowood Witch was the biggest event their village ever put on. Bigger than Christmas, spookier than Halloween – the entire village celebrated the Festival for the Twelve and it lasted for a long weekend. But it only happened once every blue moon, so she could only really remember going to a few. She knew that a witch had *supposedly* lived in Hokum House three hundred years ago, but there were lots of traditions at the festival that she'd never before wondered about – it was just the way it was always done. And she did like the cookies!

But she didn't know why the parents in the village all recited the names of their own children, or why twelve names that were etched into the stones around Hokum House were read out while everyone bowed their heads.

She didn't know why a ring of salt was poured round the house.

Nor did she know why everyone had to wear green . . .

There was so much about it that Ivy didn't know, but Maggie was fascinated by the legend, and she would throw herself right into the spirit of the festival. She baked cookies, she dressed head to toe in the brightest green, and she always, *always* put herself forward to be one of the kids who was chosen to read out one of the twelve names. She'd put her name down again for the upcoming festival.

'On a scale of I'll-Probably-Be-Fine to I'll-Definitely-Faint, how scary is this legend?' Ivy asked, wringing her hands after the final bell went to let them out of school and they made their way down the road to the library.

Maggie raised her eyebrows. 'Honest answer?'

Ivy thought for a moment, then nodded.

'Probably somewhere in the middle. Around a You-Might-Not-Get-To-Sleep-Tonight. Or, You'll-Never-Trust-A-Woman-In-Pointy-Shoes-Again.'

The library was in an old, rickety Tudor building. Maggie opened the ginormous wooden entrance door and stood back to let Ivy in first, but Ivy hesitated, her eyebrows knitted together.

'Why wouldn't I trust a woman in pointy shoes?' she asked as her glasses fogged up from the warmth of the library.

'All witches wear pointy shoes,' Maggie scoffed. 'Everyone knows that!'

'Back again, Maggie?' said Mrs Moody, the head librarian, as they shuffled inside. She was a kind lady whom Maggie and Ivy both adored. 'It's actually a good job you're here too, Ivy! That new book on theoretical physics you ordered has come in.' She wore half-moon spectacles that sat on the end of her nose and she had the longest hair of anyone the girls had ever seen. It was wavy and grey and tumbled all the way down past her hips. She usually wore green floaty clothing that billowed behind her as she walked around the library with her book trolley.

'Thanks, Mrs Moody, but —' Ivy gulped — 'we're actually here to read the legend of Crowood Peak.'

Mrs Moody looked straight at Maggie and smiled kindly. 'Will you ever tire of reading that old thing?'

'Never, Mrs Moody! But Ivy here has never properly read it, and, as the festival is coming up, I thought it would be better to show her the actual legend instead of trying to rehash it for her myself.'

Mrs Moody peered at Ivy over the top of her spectacles. 'You don't know the legend, duckling?'

'I just . . . don't know it in great detail, that's all,' Ivy replied.

'Well, we can certainly help with that!' the librarian said loudly, causing a few readers to look up from their books, but none of them dared shush the head librarian herself. 'Come over here, ducklings!' Mrs Moody floated over to the back of the library with Ivy and Maggie in tow, humming loudly as she went.

Maggie and Ivy tried not to giggle and add to the cacophony. People between the bookshelves were now tutting at the humming, and glaring at Mrs Moody.

She led them to the very end, where a big book, opened to a specific set of pages, sat inside a glass case. The book was very old, its leather coverings crinkled and weathered and its pages yellowed and beginning to crumble at the edges. The writing was in the swirliest, most beautiful handwriting Ivy had ever seen, and it was jet-black and hadn't faded at all, despite the book's age.

'Here it is!' Mrs Moody said with a flourish of her hands, like she was pretending to be a magician's assistant. 'In the old records of the village. *The Legend of the Crowood Witch!*'

Maggie gestured for Ivy to hop up on to the little step in front of the glass case so she could get a better look. With wobbly legs, Ivy did just that, and after a deep breath she began to read:

THE LEGEND OF THE CROWOOD WITCH

Once upon a time, the little village of Crowood Peak sat in the shadow of a magnificent mountain, which had a snow-covered peak soaring to the sky. But in the centre of Crowood Peak there lived a witch, whose powers belonged to the earth. She lived at its base in a beautiful house: a house passed down through generation after generation of a family named Arcturus.

This witch was kind and gentle. She healed those who were sick, helped bring new lives into this world, strengthened those who were weak and was a friend to all who passed her garden gate. She proved herself time and time again to be nothing but good. But this was not to last.

A powerful demon came upon her home and fell madly in love with her, craving her for his own. He was fascinated by her mossy-green hair and brown eyes, which reflected the earth magic that she drew up from the soil and the roots of trees. She smelled like rain and wood, and the demon became so intoxicated by her that he threw fits of wild jealousy when anyone in the area even so much as glanced in her direction.

People stopped visiting and asking for her help because the demon – whose heart was full of wickedness – refused to leave. He planned to take the witch to his lair in the Land of Shadows where she would be his one true love for all of eternity, and where she would be forced to obey his every whim.

The witch refused his offer, and told the demon she could never love someone whose heart and soul were so wicked and wild. In fury, he cursed her, condemning her to live with a heart and a soul even more wicked and untamed than his own so she would know the pain of being unloved and rejected forever more. She tried to resist him, but it was no use. His magic was stronger and it forced its way into the fabric of her soul and turned it sour. Her mossy-green hair turned raven-black overnight. She screamed in pain as darkness tore through the light in her heart and her head became foggy with evil thoughts.

As daylight broke, the kind and gentle witch was no more. What had replaced her was a cruel and selfish creature. She did not want to heal the sick and injured, nor did she want to give strength to anyone other than herself. Now she wanted power.

Once the witch had become steeped in evil, the demon returned. He proposed a new deal. In return for eternal life, she would go with him to the Land of Shadows, where they would rule together over his dominion. This time, she hungrily agreed. But the demon was not finished. He revealed that to complete the transformation from mortal to immortal, she would have to eat the hearts of thirteen innocent souls – thirteen *children* – before the end of the night of the next blue moon. If she succeeded, she would gain not just the years those children would have lived but also the years that those thirteen children's *children* would have lived, and the years of *their* children's children, and so on and so forth.

If she did not succeed, the darkness would consume her – she would vanish from the earth and the curse would pass to the next woman born in the Arcturus bloodline.

The witch agreed and began to cast a spell over the village of Crowood Peak. Slowly the adults began to forget their children – not only their names and their faces, but also their entire existence. It was as if their children had never been born at all. The witch knew it would be far easier to take a child who wouldn't be missed.

However, her magic did not work the same way on children. Although the grown-ups forgot their sons and daughters, the children remembered their friends. And one by one, they saw them begin to disappear.

Under cover of darkness, the witch would lure a single child into her house. The child would awake in their bed to the scent of smoke undercut with the unmistakable sweetness of sugar: a smell that rose from the chimney of the witch's house and ensnared the senses of her chosen child, who then followed it all the way to the witch's house. That child would never be seen again.

As the magic spread, the children of Crowood Peak were cast out of their homes by parents who no longer recognized them. The grown-ups couldn't understand why there were toys in their houses when they had never had a child, nor why there were little shoes at the door when there was no one small enough in their family to wear them.

With every child that entered the witch's house, with every heart she devoured and every soul she sent to the underworld, a great flash burst from the house – a flash so bright it could be seen for miles – and a dark swirling cloud began to form over the roof.

But the children of Crowood Peak fought back. On the night of the blue moon, they grouped together and kept watch under the light of the moon, until they saw the witch's chosen victim moving towards the witch's house. The children took hold of their friend and locked them in a cupboard until the morning.

The witch had taken twelve children. But her deal with the demon meant she needed *thirteen*. She had failed. So, as the blue moon sank below the horizon, the spell turned the witch to dust instantly, in one final burst of light.

This witch had no children of her own, but her brother had been blessed with twin daughters. Twin witches. One fact you should know about witches is that each witch's powers are unique. One witch might draw power from the tides, and when she comes of age at thirteen her hair will turn as blue as the depths of the ocean. Another young witch might find her strength from ash and flames, and so her hair will turn the colour of a burning orange sun. Each witch will be drawn to one of the four elements in her own way.

On the morning that the witch's nieces were due to come into their full magical powers – on their thirteenth birthday – something strange happened. The elder twin's hair suddenly turned raven-black and her eyes became black with it. She had inherited the curse of the Crowood

Witch! Her father, the witch's brother, who knew of the curse laid upon his sister, was fearful, and cast his daughter out without a moment's thought.

The witch's sister tried to stop her twin from leaving, but the new Crowood Witch fled to her aunt's old house in Crowood Peak. She was drawn to its evil legacy by the wickedness of the curse within her. As she grew into her powers, the darkness grew with her, and then, one day, the demon appeared. He told her that if she did not eat the heart of the thirteenth child by the next blue moon, she would turn to dust – just as her aunt had done – and the curse would pass on to the next female child in the Arcturus bloodline. But if she could complete the curse, then she could live forever, reigning over the Land of Shadows alongside him.

The new Crowood Witch began to concoct a spell to lure a thirteenth child to its doom. Little did she know, however, that her sister had been searching to bring her home. She wanted to try to mend the broken family ties and to break the curse. The scented smoke spilled from the witch's chimney like a homing beacon, leading the girl right to the doorstep. She tried to reason with the new Crowood Witch, but it was no good – too much of her soul was woven with darkness.

As the two witches fought, purple and green sparks flew from the house. No one knows exactly what happened that night, but suddenly an explosion of purple light engulfed the entire building and there was a catastrophic *BOOM!* that echoed up the mountain.

The summit of the mountain split and cracked, and boulders as big as houses hurtled down towards the village as its peak collapsed. This, it was later said, was the evil witch's final act of revenge. If she couldn't fulfil the curse and live forever, no one in Crowood Peak could live at all.

The avalanche of rocks would have destroyed at least half the village if it hadn't been for the evil witch's sister, who used her own magic to turn the rocks to dust before they made impact – except for twelve small boulders that appeared around the house before the good witch disappeared.

At the gate of the house, a slab of rock appeared overnight, bearing a prophecy etched into the stone. It read:

Three hundred years she won't be seen,
But she'll return to claim thirteen.
The sky will crack, the earth will shake,
When the dozen's circle breaks.
But when the thirteenth moon is blue,
Two sisters, fierce and brave and true,
Will send the witch to death's embrace,
And to her final resting place.

Later, the villagers carved the names of the twelve children who had been taken by the first Crowood Witch on the twelve stones, so that they would never be forgotten.

Below the ancient text, a card had been added to the glass case by Mrs Moody. This read:

Hokum House, as it is now named, has been abandoned for three hundred years. There was no female child in the Arcturus bloodline to take the place of the last Crowood Witch after she disappeared, so the curse appeared broken. However, not a soul has dared to cross the threshold of Hokum House in all that time, and it has had no choice but to fall into disrepair, without anyone alive left to care for it. Its only resident is a cat, whose green eyes can be seen glowing within the darkness of the house. No one knows who the cat belongs to, but some say it belonged to the Crowood Witch. It has been named Ramshackle, just like the house in which it lives.

3

Bad News

'She ate the hearts of twelve children?!' Ivy said through her hands. They were covering her mouth, which was agape in horror.

'Supposedly, yes,' Mrs Moody said, smiling sadly, although her left eye twitched nervously. It seemed this was a story that made even grown-ups feel uncomfortable. 'Didn't you ever wonder who those names that we read out at the festival belonged to?' she asked, but Ivy shrugged.

'The Festival for the Twelve doesn't happen *every* year. Just when there's a blue moon. I've been to . . .' Ivy closed one eye in concentration and counted on her fingers. 'Five! Five festivals have taken place in my lifetime and I can only really remember two of them. For the rest I would have been too little. In between festivals people don't talk about it much.'

Mrs Moody nodded sympathetically. 'Yes, I suppose it's like playing Christmas songs in January – people don't want to hear them. Why should it be different for our festival? The legend of the Crowood Witch, however, is a little gruesome. I'm not convinced it's true.' The librarian started to gently guide the girls away from the book.

'Of course it's true! It's a legend!' Maggie said, pointing back to the tome.

'Well, a legend is a story that has been passed down through generations, and we often have no way of knowing where it came from. For all we know, our legend may simply be a story that parents tell their children to teach them not to talk to strangers,' said Mrs Moody.

'Then why do we have a festival if it's just made up? Seems like a big waste of everybody's time and energy, if you ask me!' Maggie folded her arms. Ivy was getting the distinct sense that Maggie wanted the legend to be true. No one loved the festival more than Maggie, and she didn't want it to be based on nothing more than nonsense.

'Maggie.' Mrs Moody bent down to look at her. 'You take more books out of this library than anyone I've ever known.'

'And?'

'You *love* stories! What's the problem with this one?'

'It's different,' Maggie said, but she wasn't sure she believed what she was saying.

'Is it? Think about your favourite story. Think about the characters in it and the world they come from. Now think about how that story makes you feel when you read it.'

Mrs Moody was right. Maggie did take a lot of books out of the library, and she owned loads of books at home too. In fact, her book collection was her pride and joy. Sometimes, after she read a book, it was all she thought about for days – the characters felt as real to her as Ivy did, and a story could make her heart swell with so much love and hope that tears spilled out of her eyes. If she could hold a week-long festival for just one of her favourite stories, she'd do it with no questions asked.

'Yeah, OK,' she said with a sheepish glance at Ivy. 'I guess I understand.'

'Besides,' said Mrs Moody, 'Crowood Peak doesn't have a very exciting history. That legend puts us on the map, so we make the most of it!'

'I guess I just wish it had a happier ending,' Ivy said, shrugging.

'But that's the thing, Ivy.' Maggie put on her spookiest voice. 'It hasn't had its ending . . . yet!'

'Oh, let's not go scaring the poor thing now,' Mrs Moody said, shaking her head.

'I'm serious, though, Mrs Moody! The prophecy in the book says: "*Three hundred years she won't be seen, but she'll return to claim thirteen.*" This year marks three hundred years since the Crowood Witch disappeared, and then this strange woman showed up last night and moved in next door and it went from being a pigsty to a house fit for royalty in a matter of minutes and –'

'You mean Amy's house? Oh, Maggie, what a lot of nonsense!' Mrs Moody wafted past them to the front desk of the library and busied herself with some files.

Maggie was about to continue explaining what they had seen the night before when Ivy put a hand on her shoulder. 'Wait . . . who?' she asked the librarian.

'Amy? You know Amy, don't you? Well, you must do, since you both live next door to her!' The librarian tittered in a high-pitched tone that sounded very unlike the Mrs Moody they knew. 'No one knows where the Crowood Witch's real house is. It's been lost for centuries, but I can assure you that it certainly isn't *Amy's* house! What a silly notion indeed!'

Maggie and Ivy exchanged a look. Whatever had bewitched their fathers, to make them forget how Hokum House used to look and believe that they knew the woman who had moved in, had also got hold of Mrs Moody.

'But, Mrs Moody . . . the biggest part of the festival is gathering at Hokum House – next door to us! – and reading out the names of the twelve children that were taken. They're carved on the stones round the house,' said Maggie.

'Stones, Maggie? What stones?' Mrs Moody's face began to change. For a moment she looked confused, not only by the girls and their persistence about the legend of the Crowood Witch, but also by the words coming out of her own mouth. Ivy suddenly had the same odd feeling that she'd had with her father: she could hear Mrs Moody's voice, but somehow it was someone else's thoughts and feelings. 'Now, it's going to get dark soon. Best you two get yourselves off home for dinner,' she said with a smile. But then a dark cloud passed over her face, and she added in a voice quite unlike her own, 'And no bothering Amy with all this Hokum House nonsense.'

'OK, Mrs Moody,' Ivy said with a sweet smile. Maggie turned to her and took a giant breath, ready to protest, but Ivy gave her a look that Maggie recognized as her I-have-a-plan face. 'Oh, I think I left something over by the book . . . back in a minute. Maggie, will you come with me?'

'Of course I can, Ivy,' Maggie said, slowly and loudly. 'It would be my pleasure. After you . . .'

Ivy gave her a nudge. 'Stop acting weird. Just be normal!' she hissed. Together they made their way back to the book with the legend.

'Look!' Ivy said, as she pointed to the note below the case that described the house. She pointed so fiercely that she left a little greasy smudge on the glass which she had to wipe away with the sleeve of her jumper. 'It says here: "Hokum House has been abandoned for three hundred years . . . not a soul has dared to cross the threshold of Hokum House in all that time, and it has had no choice but to fall into disrepair, without anyone alive left to care for it." It even says that the cat is called Ramshackle because the house it lives in is exactly that . . . ramshackle!'

'So you mean . . . it's not us,' Maggie said, leaning in closer and reading the librarian's card for herself. 'We're not making this up. It's everyone else who seems to be telling weird stories about Hokum House and Amy, whoever she is!'

Maggie looked at the book again and gasped in surprise. The note below had vanished. 'But . . . but . . . it was right there a moment ago!'

'Maggie, what on earth is going on?' Ivy reached for her friend's hand.

Maggie took it and squeezed it tightly. 'I don't know, Ivy, but whatever it is, it doesn't feel good.'

Ivy and Maggie scarpered pretty quickly and were quiet for a few minutes after leaving the library, trying to take in what had happened.

'We're not going round the twist, are we?' Maggie asked quietly. The wind was really picking up now and the sky was beginning to darken with some angry-looking clouds that seemed ready to burst at any moment.

'No. No, absolutely not,' Ivy said, again not quite believing herself as she said it. 'I think it's time to convene a meeting of the Double Trouble Society.'

Maggie pushed her fist into the air. 'YES!'

★

Crowood Peak sometimes had tourists visiting because of the legend. There weren't many, but, when they did come, the Cosy Cauldron was sure to be a pit stop on their tour. It had a spooky, autumnal vibe all year round. There were cobwebs dangling from the lighting fixtures and jars containing fake eyeballs in red liquid sitting on every table as a centrepiece. It wasn't Maggie and Ivy's first choice of location for a hot drink, but on this occasion they thought it might give them some inspiration.

'We need to go through what we know to be facts and hold on tight to them, regardless of what anyone else says,' Ivy stated firmly.

'OK. So what are the facts?' Maggie asked, before she took a big slurp from her mug, which was piled high with whipped cream and dotted with pink marshmallows.

'Fact number one,' Ivy said, twisting her saucer so that Maggie could reach the biscuit that came with her hot chocolate – Maggie had already eaten hers and Ivy knew how much she liked them. 'Hokum House looked like it had been through several natural disasters before that woman showed up last night.'

'Right. Fact number two,' Maggie said, with her mouth full. 'Neither of us had ever seen that woman before last night and she has certainly never lived next door.'

'Correct. Fact number three. Neither of us knew she was called Amy.'

'Because how could we? We've never met her!' Maggie's voice was getting higher and higher with frustration.

'Exactly. Fact number four. There was writing on a card below the book in the library that described Hokum House as being completely and utterly abandoned for three hundred years, and then it totally vanished.'

'It did . . .'

Ivy and Maggie were quiet again for a moment, both trying to find an explanation for how a written card could disappear from inside a sealed glass case without either of them noticing. Ivy took her first sip of hot chocolate while Maggie drained the dregs of gooey melted marshmallow from the bottom of her mug.

'Finally, and maybe the most worrying, fact number five . . .' Ivy stared into her mountain of whipped cream like it was a crystal ball. 'If the woman who moved in next door *is* a witch, then she's shown up exactly three hundred years since the Crowood Witch disappeared – and that can't be good news.'

Outside on the street, the brown leaves were blowing up into a frenzy as the wind began to howl, rattling the glass in the window. The lights flickered momentarily.

'Does that usually happen?' Maggie asked, looking up at the mini chandelier above their table.

'I really hope so . . .' Ivy said. 'But I think maybe it's time we went home.'

★

48

As the girls walked home, they noticed the clouds were getting darker and darker. It was only when their houses came into view that they saw that the clouds weren't clouds at all. What they were seeing was *smoke*, giant plumes of it, pouring out of the chimney and creating a sort of glittering vortex above Hokum House.

Maggie grabbed Ivy's hand and together they ran to the house's front gate and peered over it.

'Look!' Maggie pointed to one of the twelve stones. It was about the size of a small melon, and although it was covered in moss you could still make out some of the letters of the name ELIJAH BROWN engraved underneath. 'The stones are still here. We aren't making things up, Ivy. It's everyone else. They've created a different story in their heads. The witch must have done that!'

'But that's not possible,' Ivy said, looking bewildered.

'I know. I know it's not reasonable or logical, but it *is* happening. I think I'm starting to freak out a little bit.' Maggie put her hands behind her head and her breathing began to quicken.

'Maggie . . .' Ivy said, but Maggie was working herself up into a bit of a state. She had begun to pace up and down and walk in circles, talking more to herself than to Ivy.

'No, I know what you're going to say. You're going to tell me that the facts don't support my theory,' she said.

'Maggie . . .' Ivy tried again, but it was no use. Maggie was officially freaking out now.

'You're going to say that there's no way everyone's minds have been wiped and —'

Ivy dug her elbow into her friend's ribs.

'*Ow!*' Maggie cried.

'Maggie, we're no longer alone.' Ivy looked at Maggie and tried to discreetly gesture towards the house with only her eyes.

Maggie glanced in the direction of the house for long enough to notice the woman.

The woman who was apparently called Amy.

The woman who everyone seemed to know, except for them.

The woman standing in the window of the house, swirling her hands in circles in front of her.

Her fingers began to glow a vibrant purple, matching her eyes. Then, as she pointed to the skies, out of nowhere Ramshackle the cat suddenly hopped up on to the fence and began to yowl louder than any cat they'd ever heard. With a hiss, it leaped towards them, claws outstretched!

'*AAARRRGHHH!*' The girls both stumbled backwards into the road — just as a car came zooming towards them! It screeched to a halt and the driver gave a long, hard honk of its horn.

'*AAARRRGGGHHH!*' Ivy and Maggie screamed even louder.

'GIRLS!' Maggie's father hopped out of the car and rushed to them without closing the car door behind him. 'What on earth is going on?' He hugged them tightly as if they were both his daughters. (They might as well be, considering how much time Ivy spent at his house.) 'Are you OK? You could have been seriously hurt!' He brushed down their hair with his hands and kissed the tops of their heads. 'Now, what has got you both so spooked, eh?'

'It's her, Dad!' Maggie cried. 'It's the woman who lives next do—'

'Nothing, Max!' Ivy nudged Maggie a little more gently this time, but enough to get her to stop talking. 'Just a stupid game we were playing. We'll be more careful next time. Promise.' She smiled as sweetly as she could.

Max eyed them both suspiciously before letting out a sigh of relief. 'All right, as long as you're sure. Maybe play inside for the rest of the evening. Looks like there's a storm brewing.'

They looked up at the sky as thunder began to rumble overhead. Only Ivy and Maggie noticed that the smoke clouds had a purple hue.

4

Poison

Ivy and Maggie rushed upstairs to Maggie's room, taking the stairs two at a time, with Frankenstein the dog hot on their heels. Maggie turned the sign on her door that read 'ENTER AT YOUR OWN RISK' round so it now said 'DO NOT, UNDER ANY CIRCUMSTANCES, DISTURB', and she slammed the door behind them.

Maggie's bedroom was very different from Ivy's. In Ivy's room, everything had its own place and she always made sure nothing was ever out of its designated spot. Her books were alphabetized on the shelves, her clothes were neatly folded in drawers or on hangers, and her dirty laundry went straight into a hamper in the corner. She didn't have many toys, but that was because Ivy found joy in model building. She'd made models of Apollo 11; its lunar module, *Eagle*; and the Mars rover twins, *Spirit* and *Opportunity*, and she'd created a papier-mâché solar system that she'd painted and hung from her ceiling. It was a colourful and vibrant, yet immaculate, bedroom – she couldn't bear it being untidy. Neither could her father. Maggie, however, had no such worries. Everything was everywhere: several decks of tarot cards, stuffed toys that looked like mythical creatures, and books upon books – many of them about witches, vampires, ghosts, aliens and werewolves. Maggie loved the mystical and the unexplained.

'Can you at least explain the mess?' her father often said to her, sighing. Maggie always argued that it was 'organized mess', but that didn't explain how she could never, ever find anything.

'If it's possible, it's even more chaotic in here than usual,' Ivy said with her back against the door, unwilling to step into the room any further for fear of tripping over one of the many stacks of books or toys and being crushed underneath, never to be seen again.

'At least I've tidied up a bit,' Maggie said, taking off her coat and slinging it on a chair in the corner, which was already overflowing with brightly coloured clothes.

'You did not!' Ivy wailed, gesturing wildly at the chaos with both her hands.

'Did too! Well . . . maybe I didn't tidy up exactly how *you* would tidy up, but I did clear a pathway from the bed to the door. I was fed up of treading on Lego every time I got up to go to the bathroom in the middle of the night.' Maggie gestured to the floor, where there was definitely a path of sorts, but certainly not a clear one. She expertly tiptoed round works in progress – models of houses and half-finished paintings where the paint pots sat still open on the carpet – and finally made it over to her bed, which she clambered up on to reach the window. She pushed it open and hung as far out of it as she could to inspect the house next door. The wind was howling and there was a rumble of thunder above them that sounded angry and threatening. Her hair was whipped into such a frenzy by the wind that she had to hold it down with her hands to be able to see properly.

'Please let me tidy up in here. Even a little bit?' Ivy asked, already picking up books and stacking them back on Maggie's shelves in alphabetical order.

'We've got bigger fish to fry. Look!' Maggie pointed to Hokum House.

Ivy carefully made her way over to join Maggie so she could get a good look. The woman was down in the kitchen, and through the window they could see her walking back and forth with various different ingredients, pouring them into a giant glass mixing bowl and then whisking violently.

'Is she . . . baking?' Maggie asked, an eyebrow raised.

'It seems like it, but why?'

'Maybe even witches like a cupcake every now and then?' Maggie said uncertainly, her mouth starting to water at the thought of delicious cupcakes.

'We have no proof that she's actually a witch, Maggie,' Ivy replied, tutting.

'What?' Maggie's mouth dropped open in shock. 'Ivy, we *saw* her do magic!'

But Ivy shook her head. 'If you're referring to the house renovation, then yes, that was weird, but it was also dark and we were up past our bedtime, so we were tired. There could still be a perfectly logical explanation for whatever it was that we saw.'

'What about a minute ago, with her pointing her arms to set that cat on us? We could have been run over!' Maggie folded her arms across her chest, her cheeks beginning to flush with frustration.

'Maybe she's trained Ramshackle really well?' Ivy said feebly.

'In one day? Ivy, we saw her fingers glow purple! I've never seen anyone whose fingers could glow purple. I don't know what more proof you need.'

'But surely, if she really was a witch, she'd be able to magic up some cupcakes instead of baking them by hand like a normal person?'

55

'Hmm,' Maggie said, her shoulders slouching. 'OK, that's a good point,' she agreed reluctantly.

'In order to be completely convinced, I think I need to see something happen up close. Something that absolutely cannot be explained by logic or reason or science,' Ivy said.

But Maggie was distracted. 'How about something like that?' She nodded towards the house and together they stared through the kitchen window at the woman. Maggie delved into the chaos around her and triumphantly grabbed a pair of binoculars, which she brought to her eyes.

Amy – if that was her name – had fetched a bottle from a kitchen cupboard. It looked like it was made of black glass, but, as she held it up to inspect it, the bottle glowed purple as the kitchen light shone through. Amy turned the bottle in her hand and, through her binoculars, Maggie could just read its label – a label that was handwritten in beautiful cursive writing. It very clearly said: *Poison*. She gasped, then slowly handed the binoculars to Ivy, so she could see it too.

'No. *Way*,' Ivy said through heavy breaths, her pulse starting to beat at an alarming rate. 'Surely she's not going to –' Ivy dropped the binoculars and stopped speaking, stunned, as Amy measured out a perfect tablespoon and gently poured it into the mixture in the bowl. She scooped the batter into cupcake cases that were lined up neatly in a tin, but instead of putting them in the oven, she rubbed her hands together until they began to glow purple and then waved them over the raw batter. Slowly but surely, the gooey cupcakes began to bubble and rise until they turned a beautiful golden brown. Suddenly they were cooked to perfection and the sweet smell floated up and over to Ivy and Maggie, who watched on with horror from the window.

'If you don't believe that she's bad news now, Ivy, I think you might be a lost cause.'

'Well . . . well . . . we don't know that she's making poisoned cupcakes for other people, do we? She might be making something like bait for rats, or . . . or . . .'

'How many more excuses are you going to make for this woman we don't know, who is clearly an evil witch?!'

'Not all witches are bad!'

'So you agree? That she's a witch?' Maggie said.

Ivy chewed on her bottom lip. She definitely had no logical explanation for how a woman could cook cupcakes with her bare hands. She might now have to start thinking illogically in order to figure out the truth. 'OK, yes, maybe. She might be a witch,' she said finally.

Maggie nodded, pouting slightly. 'I will settle for that,' she said, happy that her friend was finally starting to see what was so obvious to herself.

'Hang on, Maggie . . . Where did she go?'

Amy had disappeared from the kitchen window but they could hear the same click-clack of her boots on the pavement outside that they had heard when she had first arrived at the house. Suddenly they heard a noise that made both their hearts plummet in their chests.

DING-DONG!

5

Poisson

Maggie raced across the messy floor of her room, treading on a piece of Lego as she went. *'OUCH!'* She flung open her bedroom door so hard it slammed against the wall, making the picture frames rattle. Instead of taking the stairs, she hopped up on to the banister and slid all the way down, something her dad was forever telling her not to do. She landed with a crash and shouted, 'DAD, DON'T –'

'Why, hello, Maggie,' a soft voice replied. Max had already opened the door and the woman from next door was standing in the open doorway of their house, holding the plate of perfectly baked and beautifully iced cupcakes. Amy's dark

59

purple lips stretched into a pleasant smile as she looked at Maggie, showing her impossibly straight and dazzlingly white teeth. Her eyes were dark and didn't look purple up close, but Ivy figured she must be able to hide the way they glowed when she needed to. Her nose turned up at the end into a point, and her hair was so unbelievably white-blonde it almost hurt Ivy's eyes to look at it.

'How do *you* know who I am?' Maggie cried.

'Maggie!' Max was aghast. 'I'm so sorry, Amy. I'm not sure what's got into her. Maggie, you've known Amy ever since you were a baby. Amy even used to babysit you when I had to work late. Now, say you're sorry for being so rude.'

'I'm not saying sorry to a witch!' Maggie scoffed.

'A . . . a . . . a *what*?!' Max laughed in a strange high-pitched sort of way. 'What on earth do you mean?'

'I don't know this woman!' Maggie gestured wildly at Amy, who remained calm and composed while Maggie's voice got louder and louder. 'You're a total stranger,' she said directly to her, 'and we know you've put a spell on everyone, but it hasn't worked on us. We know *exactly* what you're up to.'

'Maggie . . .' Ivy said quietly from her hiding spot halfway up the stairs. Maggie was right, of course, but it had occurred to Ivy that maybe it wasn't the best idea to reveal everything they knew to someone who might be able to turn them into slow-worms with a simple click of her fingers.

However, Amy didn't seem angry or disturbed by Maggie's outburst. She simply kept smiling sweetly. 'I'm not a stranger, Maggie,' she said with a voice as soft and delicate as spider's silk. 'I've been here all along. Why don't you have a cupcake and take a moment to calm down. Both of you, in fact.' Amy lifted her gaze to Ivy, still crouched on the stairs. Max was looking more and more furious by the minute.

'I'm not having one of your evil cupcakes,' Maggie said, standing up, straightening her back and planting her feet firmly on the ground, fists clenched at her sides. She looked Amy right in her eyes and said, '*I know you've poisoned them.*'

'Maggie!' Max almost toppled over with shock at his daughter's insolence. 'What an awful thing to say when Amy has been so kind to you and Ivy. She's made cupcakes specially for you both and it's the least you can do to be grateful, when I gather you've been doing a lot of snooping.'

'We haven't been snooping,' Ivy said feebly, from the safety of the stairs.

'Not my words, Ivy,' Amy said. 'I simply mentioned to Max that you've both been showing a lot of interest in me and my house and my cat today, when you don't usually pay me much attention.' She smiled. 'I can see you upstairs, you know, peering at me through the windows.' She mimed holding a pair of binoculars to her eyes. 'So I thought some cupcakes might be a nice neighbourly offering. They're chocolate and caramel. Your favourites.'

Maggie glanced behind her at Ivy, whose eyes were wide. It was true. Maggie loved chocolate and Ivy loved caramel.

'How do you know they're our favourite flavours?' Ivy asked.

'I've always known.' Amy laughed. It sounded like shards of glass clinking together. 'When you were little, Maggie, you always had chocolate around your face! And, Ivy, I always used to keep caramel toffees in my pockets in case I saw you. You could follow the trail of empty wrappers to your front door.'

'None of that is true. We don't know you, whoever you are,' Maggie said, her hands on her hips.

'And we don't *want* to know you.' Ivy finally joined Maggie in the hallway, but stood a little bit behind her.

'Girls, I don't know why you're acting this way, but it's not fair on Amy when she's being so kind. Gosh, I'm so embarrassed. I'm so sorry, Amy. I promise you we will be having a long discussion about this later.' Max fixed both girls with a hard stare that made them feel slightly ashamed.

'It's OK, Max. Please don't worry. But I'd still like to leave the cupcakes here, in case you two change your minds.' Amy presented the plate to Max on her fingertips.

Best friends have a way of communicating without using words. It only takes a meaningful look or a nudge or a squeeze of the hand or arm to know exactly what the other is trying to say. Maggie and Ivy gave each other such a look at that very moment. They both began to raise their hands, but

Ramshackle beat them to it. The cat leaped up from the doorstep on to Amy's shoulder, and pounced on the plate of cakes. Amy couldn't keep hold of the plate and it plummeted to the floor, shattering into pieces. The cupcakes flew through the air and most landed icing-side down, chocolate crumbs and buttercream smooshing into the hallway carpet.

'Ramshackle! That darn cat!' Amy said through gritted teeth, wiping her icing-covered fingers on her coat. Ivy noticed that Amy wasn't licking her fingers clean like *she* would have done if she had delicious sticky icing all over them. More proof that they were poisoned. Ramshackle didn't seem to be eating the mess on the floor either. Instead, it lifted one of its hind legs, hooked a furry paw through its collar and tried to tug it loose.

'Stop that, Ramshackle,' Amy said, gently shooing the cat out of the house. 'Away! You've had your cupcakes for the evening!'

'You feed your cat cupcakes?' Max said from where he now knelt on the floor, using bits of broken plate to try and scoop the cake crumbs off the carpet. Amy knelt too to help him.

'Oh goodness, don't laugh, Max, but yes. Whenever I make cupcakes for myself or for *friends* –' Amy glanced up at Ivy and Maggie – 'I always feel bad that Ramshackle can't have any, so I make cat-friendly cupcakes too. Made with essence of *poisson*!' Amy kissed the tips of her fingers like a chef.

'*P-p-poisson?*' Maggie asked, scrunching up her nose, trying to make sense of the word she'd never heard before.

'It's French,' Ivy said, the colour draining out of her face. '*Poisson* is French for —'

'Fish! I make fish cupcakes for Ramshackle.'

Ivy and Maggie gave each other another significant look. Was it possible they'd mistaken the word *poisson* for *poison*?

'Don't worry about this mess, Amy. These two will clear it up, won't you?' Max folded his arms across his chest.

'Yes, Dad,' Maggie mumbled, not quite able to meet her father's eye.

'Of course, Max,' Ivy said, already bending down carefully to collect broken bits of china.

'And we'll replace the plate,' Max offered.

'Oh, don't worry about it. That was an old one I was going to get rid of anyway. If anything, Ramshackle did me a favour.' Amy glanced at Ivy and Maggie and they both noticed her give a small and brief sigh.

'We know you have magic,' Maggie said defiantly, despite her father's reprimands.

'There's a little bit of magic in us all,' Amy said, shrugging. Then she flashed Max one last perfect smile and was gone.

Frankenstein bounded towards them from the kitchen, sensing food had been dropped and needed hoovering up, not with the vacuum cleaner but with his tongue.

'No! Frankenstein! Stop it!' Maggie said, desperately tugging at the dog's collar. 'They're not safe to eat!'

'Enough of that this instant, Maggie!' Max said, taking the dog – already licking icing off the end of his nose – from her. 'Now, I don't know what sort of game you two have been playing, but it ends this instant. Amy is a kind woman and you were both very rude to her just now. The two of you are going to think about what you've done this evening, and tomorrow before school I'll be marching you over there to apologize.'

'But, Dad –' Maggie began, but Max held up his hand.

'I won't hear any more about it. I'm disappointed in both of you. I thought you had more manners than that.' Max collected the bits of broken china from Ivy and went into the kitchen shaking his head, with Frankenstein lolloping behind.

Once Ivy and Maggie had hoovered up the last of the crumbs and scrubbed the carpet clean, they retreated to Maggie's untidy den.

'Did we really mistake a bottle of fish paste for poison?' Maggie said quietly, her eyes sad and dull from disappointing her father. She and her dad were as much a team as she and Ivy were. Being in his bad books always upset her.

'Possibly.' Ivy grimaced. 'But we're not totally wrong about her, Maggie. Even if she wasn't trying to poison us, we still watched her do magic. Her hands glowed purple! That's a sign of someone who could cause a lot of trouble if they wanted to.'

'That's true!' Maggie's eyes lit up once more. 'So you really think she's a witch?'

'It looks like it,' Ivy admitted.

'But which kind of witch? A good one or a bad one?' Maggie asked.

'There are good witches?' said Ivy.

'Of course there are! Glinda the Good Witch of the South from the *Wizard of Oz*. She was a friend to Dorothy and the Munchkins. Hermione Granger. Sabrina Spellman. They're good witches!' Maggie said.

'So this one could be good too?' Ivy said, although she wasn't entirely sure she believed it herself.

'Or,' Maggie said, 'she's the Crowood Witch back to claim the thirteenth child, as the prophecy states.'

Ivy nodded. 'Well . . . let's not get ahead of ourselves. First things first. We need to write down a proper list of what we already know.' She reached into her school bag and pulled out her pink spiral-bound notebook. She opened it to its first clean page, which was quite far back in the book, as Ivy liked to write down anything and everything that she thought might be useful knowledge for later. She began to list the facts they had already talked about in the cafe.

Fact 1: Hokum House was a wreck until Amy showed up.

Fact 2: We have never seen Amy before in our entire lives and she certainly never lived next door.

Fact 3: Neither of us knew she was called Amy.

Fact 4: The note in the library described Hokum House as being abandoned for 300 years and then that note vanished.

Fact 5: Amy has shown up exactly 300 years after the Crowood Witch vanished.

'OK, fact number six: Amy can do magic,' Ivy said, scrawling in her notebook as she spoke.

'Fact number seven: she's put a spell on the people in our village to make them think she's been living here for ages,' Maggie added.

'Wait . . .' Ivy looked up from her notebook, her eyes darting to and fro. Maggie could tell she was having an idea. 'Maggie. We need to get to school early tomorrow.'

'Early? Because Dad wants us to apologize to Amy?' Maggie said, already yawning at the thought of having to get up for school at all, let alone earlier than usual.

'Oh yes, I forgot about that. *Extra* early, then. Trust me,' Ivy said. 'We've got some fact-collecting to do.'

6

Children Never Forget

A mist had swept over Crowood Peak during the night and was still lurking in the early-morning light. The air felt cold and crisp and stung a little as Maggie and Ivy took heavy breaths on their scurry to school. Neither of them had slept more than a wink, and when they had, their dreams had been clouded by smoke and the sound of angry crows. They both spent restless hours reading. Maggie picked up *The Lion, the Witch and the Wardrobe* and Ivy read a book about the history of Crowood Peak, but it didn't tell her anything more than the legend in the library had.

Even Maggie's morning song wasn't as upbeat as usual.
'*Good morning, Ivy Eerie,*
My eyes feel blurred and bleary.
The day outside looks dreary,
Got no sleep so I am weary!'

Maggie yawned through the whole thing, and she didn't sing it so much as groan it.

Ivy made them toast to share on their way to school – Max had once again tried pancakes, but once again they had been inedible. Fortunately, though, as he was running late, he muttered something about them going over to Amy later to apologize, before racing off himself. Maggie hoped her father might forget about it anyway, since he seemed to be behaving so oddly. So they headed to school quickly, holding hands as they went. A loud racket made them jump and Ivy gazed up to the sky. 'Look,' she said. 'What a murder of crows!'

'What?' Maggie looked confused.

'It's what you call a group of crows,' Ivy said with authority. 'It's a great name for them, isn't it?'

The crows cawed again and Ivy and Maggie quickened their step. The smell of sugar was wafting through the air around them.

'What's ruffled their feathers?' Maggie said, wiping jam from her lips.

'I don't know, but Dad had to sweep bird feathers off the front path this morning. Something's got them spooked, that's for sure.'

The girls didn't say much else to each other the rest of the way, Ivy because her mind was racing through her plan for the morning and what it meant if she was right, Maggie because she was too busy eating and yawning. She was certainly not a morning lark.

When they reached the school gates, Mr Woodman the caretaker had only just arrived himself and was unlocking the giant padlock and chain that bound the black wrought-iron gates together. He had a box by his feet, which was filled with garlands of autumn leaves with little black cut-outs of a witch on a broom nestled between the foliage.

'Good morning, Double Trouble!' The caretaker was a kind man with a big bushy beard and glasses that made his eyes look twice their size. He was brilliant at telling old stories if you had a moment to listen. He'd also share his sandwich if you'd forgotten your packed lunch, which Maggie often did. Well, Maggie forgot to pack it or Max forgot to make it. They were both as bad as each other. Sometimes, if you asked nicely, he'd be in goal if you were one person short when playing football. He wasn't very good in goal but he was very funny when his team scored. He did funny dances and made sure he high-fived everyone, whether you were on his team or not. Everyone loved Mr Woodman.

'Morning, Mr Woodman,' Ivy said politely.

'Awnin', Ister Oodann.' Maggie stifled a yawn.

'You're here early today! Eager to learn or are you hatching a plan I ought to know about? Or are you here to help me decorate for the festival tomorrow? You know how keen Mrs Haggard is to be ahead of the game!' Mr Woodman pulled a long and warty witch's nose made out of rubber from the box. It was attached to a piece of elastic that he put over his head so his nose became the nose of a gruesome storybook witch. He cackled in a high pitch, and the girls normally would have laughed – if only they weren't so worried that a real witch might be coming to feast upon their hearts any moment now.

'Oh, we're hatching a pla–' Maggie began to say without thinking, until Ivy spoke loudly over her.

'Mr Woodman, you know where Hokum House is, don't you?'

'Hokum House, of course! Why, it's right –' Mr Woodman began, pointing in the direction that Ivy and Maggie had just come from, which, of course, was indeed the correct direction to Hokum House. However, the caretaker stopped mid-sentence, and Ivy and Maggie's eyes grew wide as they saw, for the briefest of moments, Mr Woodman's irises glow purple. He shook his head as if coming out of a trance. 'Hmmm. Hokum House?' he said, in a voice that sounded both like him and unlike him at the same time. 'No one

71

knows where it is, Ivy. You know that! It's been lost for almost three centuries.'

Ivy had let herself grow hopeful for a moment, but, sadly, it looked like she might be right after all. 'I know, Mr Woodman. I don't know what I was thinking!' she said, smiling weakly, as they stepped aside to let him open up the school.

'You coming in? You're welcome to sit in my shed while you wait for school to start. I'll be busy opening up the rooms in the school, but you can help yourself to my secret stash of biscuits if you like.' He had a shed in the corner of the school playground that sort of doubled up as his office.

'Aww, Mr Woodman! You're the best!' Maggie began to walk through the gates, but Ivy stopped her.

'Thanks, Mr Woodman. But we're waiting for someone.'

'We are?' Maggie whispered, and Ivy gave her a look that meant 'play along'. 'I mean . . . we are!'

Mr Woodman smiled in bemusement and shook his head. 'OK, girls!' he said, as he walked with a merry bounce down the path to the school.

'Who are we waiting for?' Maggie whispered.

'Everyone. We're waiting for everyone.'

And Ivy wasn't kidding. As each of their classmates arrived at the gates of Crowood School, Ivy intercepted them. Isaac Hedges was one of the first. He didn't have a wide circle of friends, but Isaac didn't seem to notice and wouldn't be the sort to care even if he did – he was far too interested in ponds and frogs and nature. As Ivy ran up to him, he was inspecting the contents of a jar that seemed to have a small amount of green frothy liquid inside.

'Hey, Isaac, quick question . . . Wait . . . what *is* that?'

'It's bioluminescent algae. There was loads of it in the bay last night. My mum took me down there to collect some, but it looks really boring during the daytime.'

'Biolumi-what?' Maggie asked, closely peering into the jar.

'It's a chemical reaction within a living organism. It's like nature's own brand of glow-in-the-dark paint,' Ivy said matter-of-factly. 'But anyway, Isaac, we have something to ask you. You know where Hokum House is, right?'

'Umm . . . yeah,' he murmured, gently swirling the liquid in the jar. 'It's only, like, the spookiest place in the village. It's on Crawley Lane, isn't it?'

'Yes, Isaac. You are exactly right. Thank you. Have a truly excellent day at school!' Ivy smiled politely but the smile faded as soon as she turned back to Maggie. In fact, Maggie noticed that Ivy was starting to look a little peaky.

'Jemima! Hey, hi – I know we don't really talk much . . .' (Jemima was only the most popular girl in school, and Ivy would usually never dare speak to her because she was practically made of gemstones and sunbeams, and although Ivy wanted to be her friend, she was simply terrified of making a fool of herself in front of her.) 'But . . . I just wanted to ask – do you know where Hokum House is, by any chance?'

Jemima flicked her shiny hair back, which was the colour of magical orange summer sunsets, looked Ivy up and down with her hazel eyes, and said, 'Don't you live right next to it? What are you? Lost?' Jemima's two best friends, Jennifer and Jamie, did their secret handshake behind Jemima as they laughed in perfect harmony.

'Yes, I know. I only needed to know if you knew,' Ivy said.

'Gosh, you're such a know-it-all, Ivy. Even if you think you know everything, that doesn't mean you have the right to quiz everyone else as they go into school.'

'Yeah, you're such a know-it-all!' echoed Jamie and Jennifer. Jemima flicked her hair into Ivy's face as she turned and strutted into school.

'Well, that was brutal.' Maggie sighed. 'Why did you put yourself through that?'

'Because it was worth it.' Ivy turned round to her, but even though it seemed to Maggie that Ivy's plan had worked, her friend still didn't seem very pleased.

'Was it? What have we found out, exactly?' Maggie asked.

'Don't you see? Think about it. Who has *forgotten* where Hokum House is? Who has insisted that Amy has been around since we were kids?'

'So far, both our dads, Mrs Moody and Mr Woodman,' replied Maggie, counting on her fingers.

'Exactly. But who still knows *exactly* where Hokum House is?'

'Apparently everyone who goes to our school and . . . oh.' The penny dropped. 'Oh no. All the adults are forgetting, but the kids aren't. Why? What makes us different?'

'I don't know, but whatever spell Amy has cast, it's only working on grown-ups. We seem to be immune.'

'Maybe she needs something stronger to work on us,' Maggie wondered aloud. 'Hey! Do you think that's why she really wanted us to eat those cupcakes? Do you think she put a spell on them that would definitely make us forget?' Maggie felt suddenly grateful she had mixed up poison and fish paste – Amy's cakes might still have been enchanted!

'I don't know. But let's make sure we never eat or drink anything she gives us. Just in case.'

'Well, I've not seen my dad eat anything Amy's given him. And she's only been here a couple of days. I doubt she's had time to visit Mrs Moody at the library, and we've not seen her anywhere near the school, so Mr Woodman won't have met her either. How is she working her spell on all the adults if she's not feeding them any kind of potion?'

Ivy paused for a moment. Maggie was completely right. Neither Max nor Bill had eaten anything that Amy had given them. She simply arrived one night and suddenly, the next morning, the adults had got all muddled up.

'Maybe it's something in the air? Something like . . .' Ivy began.

Maggie and Ivy both had the same thought at the same time.

'SMOKE!'

The bell rang and everyone walking into school quickened their step, their school bags bobbing up and down on their backs. Maggie took Ivy's hand and pulled her out of the stream of their school mates filtering down the path towards their day of education. 'We have to get back to Hokum House. We need to stop her.'

Ivy nodded. 'I agree. But . . . what can we do? We can't tell our dads because they won't believe us, and we're only kids!'

Maggie began to lead her away from school, looking over her shoulder to make sure no teachers caught them. 'I think I might have a plan,' she said, and together they ran all the way back to Hokum House without pausing for breath.

7

The Circle is Broken

The smoke from the chimney of Hokum House had now created a cloud in the sky that swirled above almost half the houses in the street. It was beginning to block out the light of what little autumn sun Crowood Peak got. Maggie and Ivy stopped for a moment to take in its magnitude. The air smelled like dead rotting leaves and burnt marshmallows. Not altogether unpleasant, but definitely not normal. Maggie went to bolt across the road but Ivy reached out and stopped her.

'Ivy? What's wrong? We have to *do* something!' Maggie pointed up at the billowing, glittering smoke.

'I know, Maggie, but . . . look.' Ivy nodded towards Hokum House, where Amy had appeared in her hooded cloak at the front garden gate. There were two crows, one perched on either side of the gate, both glaring at them, cocking their heads from side to side. Amy was staring right at them too, smiling. However, her eyes were telling them that she knew they had skipped school and were coming straight for her. She raised a hand and beckoned them with a crooked finger, but they stood still.

'What do we do?' Maggie whispered, as if Amy would be able to hear them over the whipping wind.

'I think . . . we go and talk to our neighbour. If the story Amy is sticking with is that she's simply our neighbour who has known us all our lives . . . then there's nothing to be scared of,' Ivy said, trembling. 'And once we're inside we'll say that we have some questions about her house for the festival tomorrow night. We could find out something vital for our plan to stop the Crowood Witch from claiming a thirteenth child.'

Maggie nodded, her teeth chattering, but whether that was from the biting chill of the air or from the terror of talking to someone who could turn them into rats, Ivy couldn't tell. 'You sound like you've been doing some more research on the legend.' Maggie eyed Ivy. She was usually the adventurous one, so she was surprised by her friend's determination.

'Just a little bedtime reading,' Ivy said. 'I don't want to give myself nightmares, but I thought it might help if I was as clued-up as possible.'

'So you really think the Crowood Witch is going to return?' Maggie said quietly, looking back across the road at Amy, who was still waiting patiently for them to join her.

'I'm not sure, but if we're sticking to our list of facts, Amy definitely isn't who she says she is, and we need to deal with that problem first and foremost. If it turns out that she really is the Crowood Witch . . . well, we'll deal with that problem when we come to it, shall we?' Ivy took Maggie's hand and gave it a squeeze.

'OK,' Maggie said, clenching her teeth and digging deep for more courage. 'Let's do this.'

Maggie and Ivy cautiously crossed the road and came face to face with Amy, who removed the hood of her cloak and smiled sweetly, despite the wind tossing her long white hair around her.

'Hello, Double Trouble,' she said, her voice sounding like wind chimes.

'How does she know that's what we call ourselves?' Maggie whispered to Ivy, spooked, but Ivy ignored her, refusing to look away from Amy's dark eyes.

'Hello, Amy. May we come inside? We were wondering if you had any more of those delicious cupcakes Ramshackle ruined,' she said with a smile to match the sweetness of Amy's.

Something flickered across Amy's face that was less than pleasant. For a moment, she looked concerned, but it vanished as quickly as it appeared. 'I'm sorry, Ivy. I'm not welcoming visitors inside at the moment. But I'm happy to speak to the two of you on the doorstep. Max said you'd be around to apologize for yesterday.' She gave a tinkly little laugh.

Had anyone else uttered those words, Ivy would have apologized for the intrusion and maybe even felt a little embarrassed for asking to come in. However, when Amy said it, it instantly made Ivy wonder what she might be hiding in that house . . .

'Well, actually . . . yes, we are sorry for ruining your cakes yesterday,' Ivy muttered, and Maggie nodded her head. 'And for what we said. But that's not why we came over. Maggie isn't feeling too well. So we're not at school and both our dads are at work, and we were hoping you could help.' Ivy turned to Maggie and widened her eyes at her.

'Ooooh, yeeaaahhh!' Maggie groaned and began to rub her head. 'I've got a really bad headache and I'm dizzy and I feel sick and everything's getting dark and I feel the end might be nigh and – OUCH!' Ivy had elbowed her. 'And now my ribs hurt!'

'I'm very sorry to hear that, Maggie,' Amy said with sympathy. 'Max gave me a spare set of keys in case of emergencies. Let me fetch it so you can let yourselves in. And

I could call your father for you? Let him know that . . . *you're not at school.*' Ivy and Maggie both understood that Amy wasn't stupid. She knew that Maggie was actually feeling fine and that they were most definitely fibbing.

'Why can't we come into *your* house?' Maggie asked more forcefully.

'Like I said, *I'm not welcoming visitors at the moment,*' Amy said through gritted teeth.

Ivy yanked Maggie's sleeve towards her house on the right. 'It's OK, Amy. I'll take her to my house and look after her there. I'll call my dad and let him know. I'm sure he'll understand. Thanks for trying to help.' Ivy dragged Maggie back up the long path and over to her own front door without looking back. She lifted a stone plant pot and retrieved the spare key. Once they were safely inside, they let out the breaths they'd been holding.

'Why did you ask her why she wouldn't let us into her house?' Ivy said crossly.

'We clearly weren't getting anywhere by beating around the bush!' Maggie said, sitting on the bottom stair. 'Besides, she obviously knew we were lying. There wasn't much point in keeping up the fib, now, was there?'

'No . . . no, I guess not.' Ivy sat down on the floor. 'But why wouldn't she let us in? It can't be that it's messy – not when she can tidy up with a flick of her fingers! What's she hiding?'

'Oh, I don't know. Pickling jars ready to fill with the hearts of innocent children?'

'This isn't the time for jokes, Maggie.'

'I wasn't joking,' Maggie replied gravely. 'Look, I don't know what she has in that house, but maybe it's time to do things *my* way?' She jumped to her feet and waggled her eyebrows at Ivy, who suddenly clutched her stomach.

'Why does that idea make my tummy tie itself in knots?'

'Politely *asking* to enter her home clearly isn't working, so how about –'

Ivy gasped before Maggie could finish her sentence. 'You can't seriously be suggesting we break in?!'

'No! No way! That's too far, even for me!' Maggie cried, and Ivy let out a sigh of relief. 'What I am suggesting is that we maybe . . . hop over the fence! Get a closer look in through the windows?'

'That's still trespassing!' Ivy warned.

'Oh, come on! Mr Shamble always lets me jump over the fence when my basketball accidentally goes into his garden.'

'Does he *let* you, or do you do that when he's not looking?' Ivy asked, folding her arms across her chest.

'Either way, I've never got in trouble for it so . . .'

'*Maggie*,' Ivy groaned, taking the spot where Maggie had been sitting.

'OK, OK . . . think of it this way.' Maggie paced up and down in front of Ivy, pleading her case. 'Amy is definitely up to something, and if she *is* the Crowood Witch and she's come back after all these years to claim the thirteenth child, then maybe we could actually save someone's life by being a little bit reckless.' Ivy thought about it for a moment and began to nod slowly in agreement. 'No one's breaking in anywhere. There will be no breaking of anything. It's simply a little peek through a back window. What could possibly go wrong?' Maggie added.

'I've heard that from you before.' Ivy rolled her eyes. 'Double trouble is what could happen!'

'Well, are you in? Are we doing it?'

'Yes, but let's do it quickly before I change my mind.'

'YES!' Maggie punched her arms in the air in triumph. 'Wait . . . we're doing it now?'

'This is the perfect time, isn't it? Both our dads are at work and we're already skipping school. Might as well make the most of it.'

'Wow, Ivy. I didn't expect you to embrace truancy so quickly and wholeheartedly,' Maggie said with wide eyes, astounded.

'You're sick, remember? If my dad asks, that is the story and we're sticking to it. OK?'

'Oh, absolutely!' Maggie clutched her chest dramatically and leaned against Ivy's shoulder. 'I was near death! I could see the light and was about to walk into it when Ivy rushed to my side and nursed me back to health.' Ivy rolled her eyes, but smiled at the same time. 'What? I'm just practising my story. Too over the top?' Maggie added, laughing.

'Maybe a smidge.' Ivy reached into her school bag and pulled out her trusty notebook. She flipped to a fresh clean page and wrote:

Everything We Know About Witches

'I think it'd be good to remind ourselves exactly what we already know about witches from movies we've seen and books we've read, so we know what to look out for. And if we find out anything new, we can add it to the list,' she explained.

'Great idea! OK, witches make potions,' Maggie began.

'All we know is that Amy makes fishy cupcakes . . .' Ivy pointed out.

'Maybe we haven't seen any potions yet?' Maggie suggested. 'They also fly on broomsticks,' she added.

'They have spell books!'

'They have magic wands.'

'And pointy hats.'

'And pointy shoes! Don't forget the pointy shoes.' Maggie clicked her heels together three times.

'And they often have black cats. Amy definitely has one of those.' Ivy wrote everything down as quickly as she could, and she was surprised to find she had filled almost a whole page. 'Do you think witches really eat children?' she asked, putting the tip of the pen between her teeth and chewing it nervously.

'I don't think it's a typical witch's meal. It's probably only the really wicked ones who do that. You know, the old ones who have sold their souls for immortality.'

'Amy seems young, but if she's the Crowood Witch, then she's over three hundred years old,' Ivy pointed out.

'Well, let's hope that's because she has a really strong anti-ageing cream, and not because she's been eating children's hearts. Ready?' Maggie asked, giving Ivy's shoulder a squeeze.

'No.' Ivy breathed out deeply. 'Let's go.'

It had begun to drizzle, but the smoke was still thick and the smell even thicker. They went out of the back door of Ivy's house – Amy's house was set away from the road with a long path to her front door, and she might easily spot them if they went that way. They kept low to the ground, crouching behind the newly painted white panels of Amy's back fence.

'What do you think Amy is putting in that fire to make that kind of smoke?' Ivy asked, peering above them at the shimmering plumes.

'Maybe she's cooking the cat?' Maggie said, grinning devilishly.

'That's a terrible thing to say,' Ivy said, with little conviction.

'Are you seriously telling me you'd miss that evil feline?!'

'No, I wouldn't miss it – but I also don't want to see it burned alive, thank you very much! Sometimes I wonder if you're a little bit witchy yourself,' Ivy said with a prod of her finger.

'Rude.' Maggie wrinkled her nose. 'Any sign of her?'

'I'm not looking! Why don't you look? This is your plan, after all.'

'Fine . . . *three, two, one.*' Maggie quickly stood on her tiptoes and poked her head above the fence for a split second.

'Anything?' Ivy asked.

'No sign of Amy, so I bet she's in her kitchen at the front. If we can get close enough, we should be able to get a good look inside the back rooms.'

Ivy nodded and began to wiggle the panels in the fence.

'What are you doing?'

'One of these is loose. Remember Frankenstein broke it years ago when he came over here and was chasing Ramshackle out of the garden? They went right through it, but it must have fixed itself when Amy worked her magic on the house,' Ivy said huffily.

'OK. New plan,' Maggie whispered, tightening her ponytail. 'Hoist me over the fence and I'll go and look.'

'You can't go alone!'

'I have to! The fence is too tall for both of us to get over it easily, and I'm pretty sure you don't want to be the one nosing about.'

86

'OK, give me your foot.' Ivy laced her fingers together to create a foothold for Maggie to step into. Before she knew it, Maggie had pulled herself up and over, and there was a soft thud as her feet hit the grass on the other side. 'I'll just be a moment,' she whispered through the fence.

Ivy stood as high as she could to peer over the top of the panels. She saw Maggie run as quickly as she could, stooped low to the ground, over to the nearest window. But there was a curtain pulled across the lower half and it was no use – Maggie couldn't get up high enough to see in. The window on the other side of the house had thick shrubs – *prickly*-looking shrubs – right up to the windowsill. Suddenly Maggie's brown eyes appeared over the top of the fence again.

'What do I do? I can't see in and . . . er . . . now I'm stuck on this side!'

'We haven't thought this through properly.' Between the noise of the wind and her heart thudding in her ears, Ivy could barely hear herself think. The rain was coming down harder now and was making it difficult for her to see through her glasses.

'Wait! I've got an idea!' Maggie ducked out of view and Ivy could hear her moving about on the other side of the fence. 'I can see a big old stone just here. If I can get it . . . over . . . I can stand on it and look through the top half . . .' She grunted between words, trying to drag the stone out of its mossy, muddy pit. The sky had become so dark with the smoke billowing from the chimney of Hokum House that it felt like night was falling. Amy must have been stoking a fire as big as the bonfire lit every year on the village green on Bonfire Night.

'I've got a really bad feeling about this, Maggie,' Ivy said, a memory stirring in her mind.

'It's OK! I can manage on my own! It's actually not that heavy now that I've got it off the grass,' Maggie reassured her, her voice further away now, as she managed to pick the stone up and waddle with it to the house.

'No, it's not that. It's something else. Something to do with the legend, but . . . I can't quite remember. Just give me a second.'

'Well, you keep thinking. I'm almost at the house!' Maggie dropped the stone on the ground right underneath the window. Careful not to slip on its slick, mossy surface, she placed one black school shoe next to the other and went on to her tiptoes to see inside the house.

'*Three hundred years she won't be seen, but she'll return to claim thirteen.*' Ivy recited the prophecy in her head, not able to shake the feeling that she was missing something very important indeed. '*The sky will crack, the earth will shake, when the dozen's circle breaks . . .* The dozen's circle . . . ?' Ivy's heart began to pound even louder, as if it were trying to warn her from inside her ribcage. *No!* There was nothing for it. She was going to have to run through Amy's front garden and down the side of the house to Maggie's rescue.

Before she could rethink it, Ivy took off as fast as she could, down the side of the house, through the gate, then into Amy's front garden. She ran along the long path, then along the side of the house where she could see Maggie, who was peering with great intent into Amy's window. Ivy ran to the now-empty spot by the fence where Maggie had found the stone. Further up the fence was another. And then another a little further along. There would be twelve in total, she knew, looping all round the house. Twelve, including the one that Maggie was now standing on.

'Maggie! Maggie! Get down!' Ivy ran to her and tugged on her sleeve until Maggie wobbled and stepped back off the stone. Ivy knelt to inspect the stone.

'What are you doing?' Maggie protested. 'I was getting a really good look inside! I can't see any spell books but there are an awful lot of bottles that look like they could have contained potions. Well . . . either that or they're empty fizzy drink bottles, but –'

'Maggie . . . look . . .' Ivy's hands were trembling as she scraped back a handful of moss to reveal something etched into the surface of the stone.

'*Clarence Cauldwell?*' Maggie read.

'He's one of the twelve children who got taken by the Crowood Witch. This stone is part of Crowood Peak.

Remember? The witch split the mountain into pieces and sent huge boulders hurtling towards Crowood Peak. If it hadn't been for the witch's sister, the village would have been crushed! And so the people took twelve of the smaller stones and carved the names of the twelve children on to them and placed them round Hokum House. This is one of them.'

'Yeah, I know that. So what?' Maggie shrugged, wiping rain out of her eyes – rain that was coming down in huge globs that made a thwacking sound when they hit the ground around them.

'So . . . they were in a perfect circle round the house. And now that circle is . . .'

'Broken . . .' Maggie said, beginning to tremble.

'*The sky will crack, the earth will shake, when the dozen's circle breaks . . .*' Ivy whispered to Maggie.

'We've broken the dozen's circle. But . . . but . . . what does that mean?'

The sky above them cracked and sizzled with lightning – lightning that seemed to be coming from within the cloud of smoke, lightning that was the same colour as Amy's eyes.

Suddenly those eyes were upon them as Amy threw open the window, glowing so brightly that neither Ivy nor Maggie could look directly at them.

'WHAT HAVE YOU DONE?!' Amy slammed her balled-up fists against the windowsill and a shock wave of intense purple light burst from them, sending Maggie and Ivy hurtling through the air and on to their backs on the grass. Ivy looked over at Maggie and, through blurred vision, saw her lying unconscious on the grass with her eyes closed, before the darkness came for her too.

8
Inside Hokum House

Maggie's head was pounding as she came round. Her skin felt warm and tingly, like she'd just got out of a scorching-hot bath. Her heartbeat pulsed all the way through her body – she could even feel it right at the tips of her toes. As she stretched out her fingers, Maggie realized she should be feeling grass beneath her. She last remembered being outside, in the garden at the back of Amy's house. But now she felt cold, weathered leather under her hands. She opened her eyes and it took a moment for her vision to adjust to a black-painted ceiling. Panic settled in quickly as she realized she was not in her own house, or Ivy's, for that matter. This was not a place she recognized at all. With her nerves fizzing, she sat up quickly. Too quickly, and her head gave a painful throb.

'Ouch.' Maggie clutched her skull, feeling like her brain might fall out of it any minute. The leather beneath her was part of a brown sofa that had definitely seen better days. The room was dark and gloomy – the curtains were drawn – but the place looked well cared-for. There was not a single cobweb in sight. She squinted through the darkness and noticed bookshelves next to the sofa filled with mostly normal books, but every now and then a title jumped out at her like *Spells for Ne'er-do-wells*, *Magic for the Tragic* and *Craft for the Daft*. Finally, Maggie's eyes settled on a figure seated opposite her in the darkness.

The figure moved and Maggie's heart began to pound in her chest, almost loud enough to drown out the noise in her brain that was shouting: *RUN! IT'S THE WITCH!* The figure clicked her fingers together, magically illuminating a lamp, and Maggie saw Amy's face.

'*ARGHHHH!*' Maggie scuttled to the edge of the sofa, bringing her knees up and covering her face with her hands.

'Don't move too quickly. You might have a concussion. That was quite a tumble you took. You've been asleep for hours.'

Maggie peered through her fingers and then rubbed her eyes to make sure she wasn't seeing things. Amy was sitting opposite her in a green velvet armchair, holding out a black china teacup filled with something that smelled sweet and floral. 'Camomile tea, I promise. No spells or potions. Just a little dribble of honey added.' Amy crossed her heart, then placed her hands in her lap. Her voice sounded different. Softer and more relaxed. She wasn't smiling her thin smile as much either, which made Maggie feel a little more at ease.

'Where am I? And where's Ivy? What have you done with her?!' A pang of panic shot through Maggie as she quickly scanned the room. Then she saw Ivy's feet poking out from behind an armchair. The chair was facing the other way.

'You're in Hokum House, and don't worry, Ivy is fine. She's sleeping like you were a moment ago. You both fell back pretty hard.'

'Yeah, no thanks to you.' Maggie folded her arms across her chest and turned her head away from the china teacup, refusing to take even a sip, despite the fact that it smelled delicious and her mouth was ever so dry.

'I know. I'm sorry. I panicked. I'm . . .' Amy sighed, putting the cup down into its saucer on the dark oak coffee table. 'I'm not very good at controlling my magic.'

Maggie felt her heart stop its thudding for a moment . . . before it continued thumping in double time. 'M–m–magic?' she stuttered, as Amy gently chuckled. 'So it's true?'

'Don't tell me you didn't know? I know you've been on to me this whole time. I'm afraid I wasn't as subtle as I had hoped. Then again, I didn't have time to cover my tracks as well as I would have liked.' Amy looked down at her spell-wielding hands clasped neatly in her lap.

'You really *are* a witch?' Maggie whispered.

Amy looked at Maggie with her purple eyes. She seemed to be searching for something before she said, 'Yes. I am a witch, but . . . not a very good one, I'm afraid.' She nudged a plate of sugar-coated biscuits towards Maggie, who tentatively took one but didn't bite into it.

'Why not? We watched you do . . . all this. That seems like pretty powerful magic to me!' Maggie said, gesturing around her at the house they had seen Amy conjure up from a dilapidated old ruin. She heard her tummy give out a loud gurgle. She really was starving, so she broke the biscuit in half, suspiciously inspecting the inside for crushed spiders or beetle wings.

'Those are simple spells, really. Fixing a roof and painting some walls hardly takes elegant, expert-level magic.' Amy smiled a little sadly, looking around the house at her handiwork. 'My magic isn't powerful enough for much more.'

Maggie looked back up at the bookshelves and realized the books for the tragic and the daft were there because Amy thought herself tragic and daft. She felt her heart twinge

95

with guilt. She'd thought and said some unkind things about Amy, and she now suspected she hadn't been right about her at all. But she knew she still had to be careful.

'So you're not evil?'

'Far from it,' Amy said, smiling kindly.

'But you are a witch?' Maggie raised an eyebrow.

'Yes, but not every witch is evil. Those are just old stories – witches have been misrepresented a lot. There are good and bad witches, just like there are good and bad people, and lots of us are something inbetween. It's all about how you choose to use your talents.'

'Oh, I know that. There's Glinda the Good Witch and Hermione Granger and –'

'My, my! You've been doing a lot of research!'

'Well, we thought you were the Crowood Witch come back to claim the thirteenth child, and so we were trying to find out as much as we could in case we needed to stop you. But now that we know you're a *good* witch, we don't need to! And I've got to say, I'm pretty chuffed, really. I was starting to get worried that I might need to sleep with one eye open because I quite like my heart and would like it to remain in my insides rather than your . . . insides . . . Is everything OK?' While Maggie had been chatting away, a few tears had escaped down Amy's cheeks and now they were pouring out of her eyes. She started making a choking, heaving, sobbing sound that she seemed unable to control. Was she . . . laughing?

'What's going on?' Ivy began to stir in the armchair on the far side of the room. 'Where am I? Maggie? MAGGIE?!' Ivy jumped to her feet and spun round, searching for her best friend. Maggie gasped at the sight of Ivy and then burst out laughing too. Ivy rushed to Maggie's side and threw her arms round her. 'I'm so glad you're OK! I had the worst nightmare! I dreamed that we broke the dozen's circle and then we got hit by a bolt of purple lightning and – why are you laughing? What's so funny? And what in heaven's name is wrong with your hair?'

'*My* hair?! I'm laughing at *your* hair!' Maggie had begun to shake with uncontrollable giggling.

'I'm afraid it's both of your hair,' Amy said, wiping her eyes on the long, draping black sleeves of her dress. 'It seems that when I saw you'd broken the dozen's circle and panicked, I struck you both with an accidental blast of magic, which has . . . um . . . well . . . there's a mirror over there. Why don't you go and see for yourselves?' The girls looked at each other and then raced over to the corner of the room, where a large and beautiful full-length mirror with an ornate frame hung on the wall. It was big enough that they could stand side by side and still see the whole of themselves reflected in it.

'No way!' Maggie said, admiring her new look.

'My dad is going to *kill* me,' Ivy said, covering her mouth in shock but not able to look away, because the two girls staring back at Maggie and Ivy out of the mirror both had bright purple hair!

Maggie took out her hair bobble and let her hair – which used to be straight and black – fall around her face. 'Is it just me or is it kind of . . . glowing?' She cupped her hands, making a little cave round the ends of her hair, and stared inside to confirm that her hair was giving off a little light.

'Oh, great. Not only do I look like a character in a pre-school TV show but now I also glow in the dark?' Ivy said moodily, pulling her scruffy plaits out in front of her to get a better look.

'Look on the bright side!' Maggie grinned, bumping Ivy's shoulder with a balled-up fist.

'Which is?'

'You've always been scared of the dark. Now you're your own nightlight!' Maggie said, giggling.

'Urgh!' Ivy groaned. 'Wait a minute . . . where are we?'

'You're inside Hokum House,' Amy said softly. Ivy gulped and slunk behind Maggie. She'd not had time to take in her surroundings, and now that she was over the shock of waking up with a less-than-desirable hair colour, the panic was starting to sink in.

'Don't worry, Ivy,' Maggie said, sounding certain now. 'She's not the Crowood Witch. She's one of the good ones. I'm sure of it. She's . . . in fact . . .' Maggie turned to Amy. 'Who exactly *are* you?' Then she took Ivy by the hand and led her over to the sofa, where she retrieved her biscuit, ate one half and handed the other to Ivy. Ivy sniffed it suspiciously and nibbled the edge, politely putting it on a wooden coaster on the coffee table.

'My full name is Amethyst Arcturus, but you can still call me Amy if you want.' Amethyst poured herself a cup of tea by simply wiggling a finger. The black teapot lifted itself into the air and poured the tea into an empty teacup.

'Arcturus? Like . . . like in the legend?' asked Ivy.

'That's right. The family that was cursed by a demon. That curse has to be fulfilled – or halted – or it will keep passing from generation to generation.'

'But if the curse didn't pass to you, and you're not the Crowood Witch, then who is?'

Amethyst took a sip of her tea and gave a satisfied '*Ahhhh!*' afterwards. 'Well, *I* am certainly *not* the Crowood Witch,' she assured them. Then she reached up to her neck, where there was a little oval-shaped locket with a green gemstone set into the front. She closed her hand round it and pressed it tightly to her chest. 'But I am the Crowood Witch's twin sister – and I've come here to stop her from claiming the thirteenth child.'

9

Emerald and Amethyst

'The Crowood Witch is your sister?' Ivy said. Her voice was barely audible, but the room was so quiet Amethyst heard her and nodded her head.

'Yes. Her real name is Emerald and she's my twin sister.' Amy wasn't able to meet their eyes.

'But wouldn't that make you centuries old?' Maggie asked, reaching over to eat another one of the biscuits Amy had offered her. It was delicious.

'Three centuries, to be precise,' Amy replied, sipping her tea.

'But you look so young . . .' Ivy said, gesturing to Amy's long, flowing blonde locks. 'Y-y-you didn't eat the hearts of any children, did you?'

Amy spluttered, choking on her tea. 'No! Oh my goodness, no! I would never do such a despicable thing. But when I saved Crowood Peak from being destroyed, I banished my sister with a special kind of magic: a magic that bonded us and has kept us both alive for all this time. It's been a very, very long three hundred years.' Amethyst closed her eyes for the longest moment. Maggie and Ivy thought she'd gone to sleep right there and then, but then her purple eyes snapped open again and Amethyst was back in the room.

'Wait, wait, wait. I'm confused.' Maggie rubbed her forehead – she still had a bit of a headache from the blast of Amy's magic. 'Your aunt was cursed by a demon and then made a deal with him to become immortal and rule beside him, right?' Maggie asked.

'Sadly, that is true, yes.'

'But she didn't succeed in eating the hearts of *thirteen* children, correct?' Ivy added, twisting the ends of her messy purple plaits between her fingers as she spoke.

'That is also true. You really have done your homework.'

'And now your sister – who has inherited the curse – has to eat the heart of the thirteenth child by the next blue moon in order to complete the deal your aunt made? But there have

101

been loads of blue moons in the last three hundred years! How is it that your sister has survived until now?'

Amy blinked quickly at the girls, then shook her head and sighed, resting her teacup on the table. 'That would be my doing, I'm afraid. I put a time spell round this house. Anyone who lives within it will not age a day. Even you two. While you're in this house, you will remain stuck at the ages you are.'

'Couldn't the first Crowood Witch . . . I mean . . . Emerald have just cast a spell like that in the first place?' Ivy asked. 'She'd have been immortal then, without needing the demon.'

'Those sorts of spells only work on small, clearly defined locations. I could encase this house, but no further. Emerald wanted to travel and rule the entire world. No one has magic strong enough to take a spell like that with them wherever they go. Not even Emerald.' Amy reached up to her necklace once again.

'Why would you want your sister to live for so long if she's so evil?' Maggie asked, reaching for another biscuit.

Amy shrugged helplessly. 'She's my sister. I had hoped that maybe I would be able to make her see sense, change her wicked ways – but even in banishment she was impossible.'

'So how have you stayed so young for three hundred years?' Ivy asked.

'Like I said, the spell I cast binds us together. It works even better because we're sisters; we share blood. There's a piece of her magic in this locket, keeping me young like her, and she wears a piece of my magic too, keeping her trapped in this house. They tie us together and connect us. Keeping us united until –'

'Until we broke the dozen's circle,' Ivy mumbled.

'Yes. I'm afraid that's right. I imprisoned Emerald within this house and I protected it with as much magic as I could, but my magic isn't as strong as Emerald's. Oh no. Her magic is dark and sophisticated. She can think things into existence without waving a hand or uttering a spell. She simply has a thought and it can happen. The magic I use is ancient, clunky. I'm what they call a moon witch – my magic works best under a full moon, and so it waxes and wanes and is as temperamental as the tides. I've been practising it for the last three hundred years, but when the moon isn't at its fullest, I'm not very powerful at all.' Amethyst sighed. 'We never found out what kind of witch Emerald was, as the curse took hold of her as soon as she came of age. But I always wonder if that was because she was an earth witch, like the original Crowood Witch. Her magic has always been as sturdy as the mountains and as sure as the ground beneath your feet.'

'Is the smoke your magic?' Ivy asked.

'Yes, that's my magic. It's a forgetting spell. I thought if everyone forgot about Hokum House then no one would be able to come here to break the circle. Turns out my magic wasn't quite strong enough to work on children too – it's ever so easy to manipulate the mind of an adult, but the mind of a child is made of much stronger stuff. That's what those cupcakes were for the other day. They weren't *poisoned*, but . . . they did have a little bit of a spell mixed in.' Amy fumbled her hands together over and over in her lap. 'Just a little bit of magic to make you forget about the house, and the witch too.'

'Well, I'm glad we didn't eat them. I'd rather know what's going on,' Ivy said, and Maggie nodded in agreement.

'I'm glad too, to be honest. Sharing this secret feels like a weight off my shoulders. Even if it does mean my sister is about to return,' Amethyst said, sighing.

'So we've broken the circle, one of the protective spells. Surely there must be more than the one?' Maggie began to eat the biscuits at an alarming rate, crumbs spraying from her lips as she spoke.

'There are, but now that there's a chink in the chain, Emerald will already be sensing that weakness and gaining strength. She might not know it yet, but soon she'll feel her powers returning. The prophecy states that once the dozen's circle breaks, the Crowood Witch will return.'

Maggie stopped eating and she and Ivy shared a horrified look, tears brimming in their eyes.

'We're so sorry, Amethyst,' Ivy said, her bottom lip beginning to tremble.

'Yeah. I can't believe we're the reason she's coming back. We've put everyone in danger.' Maggie dropped her head into her hands.

'A prophecy doesn't always come true, but it did warn everyone that this might happen. I had three hundred years! I should have been prepared. But that's enough of shoulda, woulda, coulda's. There's nothing to be done now except try to stop her when she does appear.' Amy tried to give the girls a smile, but she hadn't filled them with much confidence.

Ivy slowly rose to her feet and began to pace in a circle round the armchair and the sofa, her brow creased in deep thought. There was something else Amy wasn't telling them that was very important, she knew.

'Hang on . . .' Maggie said. 'You said you trapped Emerald in this house. How come we've never seen her?'

Amy laughed her sweet chiming laugh. 'Oh, my dear girls, you *have* seen her. She's been here all along.'

'She's right, Maggie,' Ivy said, looking under the sofa and around the room for something she obviously couldn't find. 'We've seen her almost every day of our entire lives.' Then Ivy started making some very strange squeaky noises with her lips.

'Figured it out, have you, Ivy? Gosh, you're clever.' Amy took a deep breath, her eyes sparkling at them both.

'Ivy, I think I would remember if I'd seen a witch every day of my life,' Maggie scoffed.

'She doesn't look like a witch, though, does she, Amy?' Ivy said.

'No,' Amy replied. 'She doesn't.'

'Then what on earth does she look like, Ivy?' Maggie asked, throwing up her hands.

Finally, Ivy's strange noises had done the trick. Ramshackle ran into the room and hopped up on to the sofa next to Maggie, the purple gem dangling from its collar glinting in the light of the lamp.

'The Crowood Witch looks like a cat!' Ivy cried.

10
The Witch Returns

Ramshackle the cat gave a low growl and a hiss as Maggie, Ivy and Amy stared at her.

'*That's* the Crowood Witch?' Maggie sneered, inching further and further away from the scraggly black cat. The cat was bony; what was left of its fur was matted and its two front fangs were permanently on display, snagged on its upper lip.

'Yes, that is my sister,' Amy replied, without taking her eyes off the feline. 'Trapped in the body of a mangy cat for almost three hundred years. I don't know how much she knows or remembers of what happened, but she still seems pretty angry to me. You can't stroke or even touch her, and she won't eat anything you give her. Even when I make her the finest fishcakes, she turns up her nose. She'll only eat what she manages to catch herself in the garden.'

'She's been in my bedroom,' Ivy whispered through trembling lips. 'Sometimes she hides under my bed before I go to sleep.'

'So all that time we were searching for monsters under the bed, we should have been looking for a *witch* under the bed?' Maggie said, looking totally stunned.

'Oh, goodness. Really? Your bedroom must fall under my protection spell,' Amy said, going to the window and peeking out at Ivy's house. Maggie and Ivy weren't sure how long they'd been asleep after their tumble, but the autumn night was beginning to fall quickly. 'When I cast that spell, there weren't houses on either side. It was mostly barren land, so your house must have been built partially within the spell's border. Sorry about that. You might be a bit younger than you think you are, seeing as you haven't been ageing while you've been asleep.'

'That spell's broken now, anyway,' Maggie said, sliding off the sofa and moving to the same side of the room as Ivy and Amy. 'So you don't need to worry about this daft cat sneaking in unnoticed any more, Ivy.' Ramshackle's body went still, its ears pricked up and its green eyes wide and alert, its gaze darting between Maggie, Ivy and Amy.

'Maggie . . .' Ivy warned, noticing that the cat was paying keen attention.

'I do feel really, really bad about breaking the circle but . . . at least that's one good thing that's come from it, eh?' Maggie chuckled gently and shook her head.

Ramshackle lifted a back leg and hooked it underneath its collar and began to tug furiously.

'Maggie, I don't think talking about this in front of you-know-who is such a good idea . . .' Amy pleaded gently.

'So if the circle is broken already and the return of the Crowood Witch is imminent, how is it going to happen?' Maggie asked.

'I think we're about to find out.' Amy moved herself between the girls and held out her arms in front of them as Ramshackle gave one final tug of its collar and finally the leather band snapped. The purple gem that once hung from Ramshackle's collar flew into the air, catching the light as it spun and tumbled into Amy's outstretched hand.

Ramshackle fixed Amy with a hard stare, threw back its head and let out a human cackle. It laughed hysterically, like it hadn't laughed in three hundred years, and didn't stop. Suddenly the cat's back hunched at a disturbing angle and gave out a hideous crack that echoed around the room. Then, one by one, its legs bent in ways they shouldn't bend and the bones sounded like they were being broken into several splintering pieces.

'OUT OF THE HOUSE, NOW!' Amy screeched as she grabbed the two girls by the backs of their school jumpers, practically lifting them off their feet and carrying them into the garden.

'What's happening?' Maggie squealed as they ran down the path, scrambled through the gate and out into the road in front of Hokum House. Amy reached into her boot and produced a long black wand. It had a purple gem on the hilt and there was a natural knot in the wood a few centimetres above where her index finger wrapped round it.

'You just told the Crowood Witch that the main spell protecting this house had been broken!' Ivy squawked.

Maggie threw her hands up to her mouth, but it was far too late for that. The cat was out of the bag. Or, rather, the witch was about to be out of the cat.

'Now, now – let's not place any blame here,' Amy said, brandishing the wand in front of them all. 'This is a prophecy that was written centuries ago. This was going to happen sooner or later.'

Ramshackle let out a shriek of either pain or delight; none of them could tell.

'Yes, but later would have been better than right now,' mumbled Ivy. 'What is going on in there?'

'The transformation from animal to human is never a pleasant one, but Emerald has been in that form for almost three hundred years to the day. That's bound to make it a little harder and a lot more painful to become her human self again.'

'What happens when the transformation is complete?' Maggie asked, as the windows of the house began to glow green and the sky began to get even darker.

'I don't know, girls. I really wish I did.' Amethyst held out her hands either side of her for the girls to take. Maggie and Ivy shared a look: if the Crowood Witch was about to return, Amethyst was their best hope of getting rid of her again. Together, they nodded and silently decided between them to take Amethyst's hands. Her long, slim fingers were ice-cold as she squeezed their warm palms against hers.

Suddenly, there was a scream so loud they had to let go again to cover their ears. Then the scream turned to laughter. It was a laugh filled with a mischief so dark and cruel it made Maggie and Ivy tremble.

'She's back,' Amethyst whispered. 'The Crowood Witch has finally returned.' The shrieking from within the house grew louder and more ear-piercing, until finally a great flash of green light burst through the roof.

'Amy, your spell!' Ivy tugged at Amethyst's long sleeve, hiding behind her and peering with one eye past her shoulder at the gaping hole in the roof. 'The spell in the smoke. Now that the Crowood Witch is back, we need everyone to remember her. Hokum House too.'

'She's right,' said Maggie, shivering. The temperature had dropped and Maggie and Ivy wrapped their arms tight round themselves. 'We need as many people as possible to be on our side and to fight with us against her.'

'OK – stand back, girls.' Amethyst rubbed her hands together, creating a purple glow. She began to mutter something under her breath, and then, with a great flourish, waved her hands at the smoke cloud swirling above Hokum House, still billowing from the chimney. A weak beam of light came from her hands but barely reached the smoke. The green light coming from the house was like a theatre spotlight, cutting through the dark with ease. The purple magic coming from Amethyst's hands was like a feeble torch losing battery power with every second.

'No, no, no,' Amethyst muttered, rubbing her hands against her coat and trying again, but to no avail.

'Amy, what's wrong?' Ivy asked.

'My magic. It's not working and I don't know why,' Amethyst wailed. She kept muttering and waving her hands, scrunching her eyes shut, but her magic did not get any stronger. 'I can't do it.' She let the magic in her fingertips snuff out completely and dropped her arms by her sides in defeat.

'Poor little Amethyst,' a voice boomed all around them, coming from every direction at once. Maggie and Ivy wheeled round, trying to work out where the voice was and how the witch had escaped from the house unnoticed.

'It's a trick, girls. A distraction. She's still in the house,' Amethyst explained, not taking her eyes away from Hokum House.

'Three hundred years to practise, and your spells still aren't up to scratch? Whatever have you been doing over the years?' sneered the witch's voice. 'I, on the other hand, have been biding my time, storing up every ounce of power I have, and now you'll *never* be a match for me!' she crowed. Then Emerald let out a cackle so piercing that every window in Hokum House shattered.

Amethyst threw her arms round Maggie and Ivy, shielding them from the shards of glass that shredded the air. When it was safe, she moved back to reveal the Crowood Witch herself, floating above the hole in the roof, shrouded in smoke and green light. Emerald had hair so dark you almost couldn't see it against the black of the night that had fallen around them. Tendrils flowed out around her as though she was suspended in water, and her dress was covered in matted black fur. Her bare feet were dirty and her toenails and fingernails were long and curved like the claws of a cat. But what rooted Maggie and Ivy to the spot were her eyes. Not only were her irises black, but so were the whites of her eyes. The curse of the Crowood Witch had turned her insides as black as the charred pits of Hell itself.

'You'll rue the day you broke the dozen's circle, Maggie Tabitha Tomb and Ivy Maple Eerie! Because of you, I will eat the heart of the thirteenth child and finally reign supreme, FOREVER!'

Emerald let out one last blood-curdling cackle and a green blast burst across the sky. Crows shot up into the air from their perches and took flight; the noise of their wings flapping sounded like fireworks exploding through the sky. The smoke that had been black and glittery purple turned a putrid shade of green. The witch flew off through the air and Maggie, Ivy and Amethyst followed the green smoke trail in the sky. A small hope that Emerald might be leaving, that they'd never see her again and that she'd be someone else's problem to deal with, grew in their chests, but that hope fizzled out when they saw the smoke trail finish at the summit of Crowood Peak itself. Three hundred years after Emerald had splintered the rock and sent it tumbling towards the village, she was back – and now she was returning to set up camp.

Amethyst raced inside the house with Maggie and Ivy quick on her heels. It was a mess. There was glass all over the floor and the furniture, not to mention a couple of disgruntled birds who, having made their nests on the roof, had fallen through when Emerald made her grand exit. Amethyst ran to the fire in the hearth and emptied the contents of a small nearby cauldron over it to extinguish the faintly fluttering flames.

'I don't suppose that will help much, but it's better than nothing,' she said, sighing.

'Oh, Maggie, look!' Ivy pointed out of the glassless window. Two cars had pulled up either side of Hokum House. 'It's our dads! They'll be expecting us home for tea about now.'

'I reckon my dad's gonna love my hair like this!' Maggie swished her hair around like she was a rock star standing in front of a wind machine.

'Maggie. Perspective. Please. We've just watched a cat turn into a witch, half destroy a house and promise to eat a child's heart so she can live forever side by side with a demon! The last thing I'm worried about is what my dad will think of my hair!' Ivy put her hands on her head, trying to cover up as much of the vibrant colour as she could.

'Why don't you like it? You *love* bright colours, like pink!' Maggie said, tugging Ivy's hands away.

'Firstly, this is purple. Secondly, I might like the colour pink but that does not mean I think that colour belongs on my head. Sorry, Amy. I know you didn't mean it, but . . . I do not like this.'

'I can try to fix it if you want?' Amy raised her hands, which seemed to spark like she was short-circuiting.

'Nope! I'm good! Happy to buy some hair dye with my pocket money. That should fix the issue without any further risk . . .'

'Come on, Ivy.' Maggie grabbed Ivy's hand and led her to the front door, now hanging off its hinges crookedly. 'Better face the music! We'll come back first thing tomorrow and figure out a plan, Amethyst,' she shouted over her shoulder.

'What about school?' Ivy asked, horrified at the thought of not attending for a second day in a row.

'As important as school is, I think Maggie is right,' Amethyst said, wringing her hands. 'We need a plan. Anywhere that lots of children are together might be the first place Emerald goes.'

'Yeah, and not getting my heart eaten by a three-hundred-year-old witch is slightly higher on my list of priorities than learning maths,' Maggie said.

'Fair point,' Ivy said, with a nod. 'Tomorrow, first thing,' she added as they scrambled out of the door towards their fathers' cars.

Maggie caught up with Max first and ran straight into his arms. 'I'm so glad you're home! It's been such a weird day! So much has happened and I know you don't remember everything about Hokum House and the witch, but I do need you to trust me because –'

'Whoa, whoa, whoa!' Max gently took Maggie's hands from round his waist. 'Excuse me!' he called to Amethyst, who was still standing in the doorway of Hokum House. 'Is this your daughter?'

Maggie stumbled backwards away from Max as if she'd been struck across the face.

'My daughter?' Amethyst repeated, joining them at her front-garden gate.

'Yes. You really ought to teach her about stranger danger. She came right up to me and hugged me as if she knew me! I could have been anyone! You gotta be careful, kid!' Max opened up the boot and took out his backpack and slung it over his shoulder. He began to walk towards his home, but Maggie ran in front of him, her arms spread wide to block his path.

'Dad! It's me! It's me, Maggie. Your Maggie. I'm *your* daughter.' Maggie's eyes had begun to fill with tears and Ivy feared one more word from Max might send her over the edge.

'Max? Is everything OK?' Bill, Ivy's father, walked over from his own car to see what the commotion was.

'Dad? You remember me, don't you?' Ivy asked quietly, knowing already what the answer would be.

'Oh, I'm sorry, I don't have time for any pranks today, I'm afraid. I've got to focus as I've almost finished my new invention! It's a toaster that will never burn toast. Imagine that! Perfect toast every single time!' Bill grinned, his eyes glazed over. 'Are you lost? Can I help at all?' He looked perturbed at the thought of two lost children, but seemed completely unaware that one of those children actually belonged to him.

'No, it's OK. Don't worry. You . . . look a lot like my dad, that's all,' Ivy said quietly as a tear rolled down her cheek.

'These are my nieces! They've come to visit their Aunt Amy for a little while,' Amethyst said brightly. She opened the gate and beckoned Maggie and Ivy back towards her house. 'And we're playing a silly game, aren't we? A game that will be over soon.'

Amethyst said the last part pointedly to the girls, who cast a glance up to the green glowing mountain that loomed over the village. They nodded miserably, then trudged in single file through the gate and back up the path to Hokum House.

'Goodnight, gentlemen,' Amethyst said sweetly, and followed the girls up the path, leaving a perplexed Bill and Max each to go home alone.

11

The Crows of Crowood

Maggie and Ivy sniffled and said nothing as Amethyst cast a spell over the house to unshatter the windows and fix the roof. Her magic was still weak, however, and although the glass was back in the window frames, it was still cracked and you could hear the wind whistling through the gaps. Later, after she had produced a normal sort of meal for the girls – fish fingers and baked beans, not a crushed beetle in sight – Amethyst used the last of her strength to magic up two pairs of dark purple pyjamas with matching slippers.

'I'll see what I can do about beds tomorrow, girls,' she said, stumbling to the armchair in the living room and collapsing into it in a heap.

'We can sleep on the sofas tonight,' Ivy said, trying to sound cheerful. 'It'll be like a sleepover.'

'What happened, Amethyst? Why don't our own dads remember who we are?' Maggie asked softly, her head bowed.

'It's Emerald, Maggie,' Amethyst insisted, her face muffled by several sofa cushions. 'This is exactly what she did last time. She casts a spell causing every parent or guardian to forget their own children. It's much easier to steal a child if no one will notice they're missing.'

'*All* the parents have forgotten their children? Not just ours?' Ivy asked.

'Unless she was planning to target you two and *only* you two,' Amethyst said, looking worried. 'But that's never really been Emerald's style. She's an all-or-nothing type of person. Go big or go home.' Amethyst yawned through her words and curled her legs up towards her, ready to settle in for the night.

'But that means every child in Crowood Peak will be without a home tonight,' Ivy said, horrified.

Maggie gasped, thinking how awful she had felt when her father had forgotten who she was, and knowing every child would be feeling the same right now. 'Parents all over the place will be kicking out these strange children they've found in their homes . . .' she whispered. Her lip began to wobble again.

Suddenly Amethyst's eyes were wide, the thought of lost and frightened children forcing her up and out of the cosy armchair and over to the window. 'Oh, goodness, girls! You're right! Look!' She pulled the curtains aside and beckoned them to the window. They peered between the cracks in the glass and the sight they saw was a sorry one indeed. The children of Crowood Peak were wandering aimlessly along the road in their pyjamas, slippers and fluffy dressing gowns, looking miserable and lost. Two girls sat consoling each other on the kerb and others angrily kicked fence posts or threw stones at their parents' parked cars.

'We can't leave them out there, Amethyst. We're the only ones who can explain to them what's going on,' Ivy pleaded.

'Maybe they can help us come up with a plan to defeat Emerald? If the adults can't help, I bet the kids will!' Maggie said.

'You're right. Come on.' Amethyst ran to the front door and swung it wide open. She rubbed her hands together, and although the most she could create was a small purple glow, she only needed a little bit of magic for her next trick. She placed her hands round her throat and drew in a deep breath. 'Children of Crowood Peak!' Her voice came out of her mouth as if it were coming out of a megaphone. It was loud and booming and seemed to travel for miles. All the children turned their heads towards Hokum House, paying close attention. 'Do not be alarmed! The Crowood Witch has entranced your parents into forgetting you, but this spell will not last forever. I am Amethyst and I am the Crowood Witch's sister. I banished her once before and I can do it again. Come to Hokum House and stay the night. I promise that you will be safe here.'

Amethyst pulled her hands away from her throat, but no one moved a muscle. There was an eerie silence that filled the street as the dead leaves rustled past in the wind and the sky rumbled over the mountain in the distance.

'They don't trust me,' Amethyst said, her voice hoarse and dry. 'Not only am I a stranger, but I'm a witch too. Why would they?'

'Come on, Ivy. These are our school friends. They'll believe *us*.' Maggie raced out of the house in her purple pyjamas and her slippers and zoomed towards the child closest to the house. Ivy recognized the girl from quite a few years below them at school. She was about five years old. Maggie took her hands and said something that made the girl's bottom lip begin to wobble violently, then together they began to walk back towards the house.

'This is Darla,' Maggie said to Ivy and Amethyst with a huge grin on her face. Darla waved her hello with one hand while holding on to a stuffed unicorn by its golden horn with the other. Amethyst stepped aside and Darla ran into the house as fast as her little feet would carry her.

'What on earth did you say to her, Maggie?' Amethyst asked.

'Yeah, she looked pretty upset,' Ivy said, peering in through the doorway to watch Darla duck behind the sofa.

'The truth! I told her that you only do good magic, that you're going to defeat the Crowood Witch, and if Darla didn't want her heart eaten, then she'd better get inside the house as quickly as possible,' Maggie stated.

'Maggie!' Ivy gasped.

'Am I wrong?' Maggie asked.

Ivy and Amethyst couldn't answer because they both knew that no, Maggie was not wrong. In fact, she was so right that the three of them ran from the house and began to spread the message to the children that the safest place for them to be was inside Hokum House. They pointed up to the mountain, where green smoke spiralled and flashes of light came from the summit like bolts of lightning. They explained that the Crowood Witch was called Emerald and she had spent the last three hundred years as a cat. They told the children that she had returned – although Maggie and Ivy decided to omit the fact that it was they who had accidentally helped her return – and now she was back, she was planning to eat the heart of one last child so that she could stay youthful for all of time and wreak havoc on the earth for evermore.

The children of Crowood Peak started to run as fast as they could. There was a sudden rush to get inside as quickly as possible. The children crammed themselves through the doorway, squeezing past one another and shouting. Amethyst waved her hands and the doorway grew wider, allowing the children inside with ease. Once the last few stragglers had made their way into the house, Amethyst returned the doorway to its original size and closed the door behind her.

Amethyst, Maggie and Ivy had expected chaos, but the children were too sad and frightened for that. Instead, they mostly found somewhere to sit, some of the younger children finding spaces to lie down or resting their heads against the older children's shoulders, and an eerie hush fell over them all. Judging by the frightened looks they were throwing at Amethyst, they were also a little scared of her. Not surprisingly, considering they'd never encountered a real witch before, and if Amethyst was anything like the witches in some of the stories they'd been told, she might turn them into toads if they were too loud or upset her! So they simply sat and watched each other, looking for signs of hope and comfort. It was almost as if they were waiting to be told what to do next.

Maggie usually wished she could have a day when she didn't have a bedtime or could eat dessert whenever she liked and not just after dinner. Now that her father had forgotten who she was, she missed the sound of him telling her it was time to turn out the lights and go to sleep, or that she couldn't have another bowl of ice cream because two was already one too many. She looked around and realized everyone probably felt the same.

'Why has the witch returned?' Eddie, Ivy's science partner, asked. Maggie and Ivy shared a look laden with guilt.

'That would be our fault. We broke the dozen's circle,' Ivy explained.

'The dozen's circle? Like . . . in the legend?' asked Isaac, who was sitting at the end of the sofa by Darla, her head and the unicorn's horn poking above the big cushion she was hiding behind. 'It's real?'

'No. The legend isn't real,' scoffed Jemima, and her friends Jennifer and Jamie nodded furiously in agreement. 'It's just a scary story to make kids behave.'

'I can assure you it is not.' Amethyst spoke up abruptly, and her voice was so firm that almost everyone jumped out of their skin. 'The Crowood Witch is *very* real. Twelve children were taken by her hundreds of years ago and now my sister, who has inherited the curse, is on the hunt for a final child to make it thirteen.' Everyone shifted uncomfortably and someone began to weep softly.

'So much for not scaring people . . .' Maggie muttered.

'But you can stop her, can't you? You're a witch too,' Isaac piped up, clutching a jar of something that looked like it was bubbling.

'Not only is Amethyst a witch, Isaac, she's the Crowood Witch's sister. But she's a good witch and, if anyone knows how to defeat Emerald, it's Amethyst. She can help us.' Maggie puffed out her chest, beckoning Amethyst forward to speak.

'I want to help. I really do, but my magic . . . it's faded and I don't know why.' Amethyst looked down at her hands and rubbed them together, trying to find the magic beneath her fingertips. 'It's not as strong as it was only a few days ago. I think my sister returning and getting stronger has made me weaker somehow.'

'You'll get stronger, Amethyst. I know you will,' Maggie said encouragingly.

'I think we . . . need some rest,' Ivy said.

'I think you all need to be locked up for spouting this nonsense,' Jemima sneered. 'I don't know about you lot, but I'm going home. My parents haven't forgotten me. They both, well . . . had a forgetful moment. At exactly the same time. That's all. You'll see.' She tightened the belt on her plush baby-blue dressing gown and stomped towards the front door.

'Jemima, you can't go outside. It's too dangerous!' Ivy pleaded.

'If you think I'm about to listen to someone with hair as hideous as yours, you've got another think coming. Purple really isn't your colour, Ivy,' Jemima snapped.

Ivy waited for everyone to laugh at her, but no one did. Even Jennifer and Jamie, both now skulking in the corner of the room, didn't utter the slightest little snicker at Jemima's cruel comment.

'Witches, really!' Jemima barked as a parting shot. Then she stepped out of the house and walked down the long path on her own. She opened the front-garden gate still muttering to herself. She turned to take one last look through the doorway in the hope that someone would be coming with her, but everyone else remained inside the warmth and safety of Hokum House. The wind really was blowing now, so much so that Jemima pulled her dressing gown round her neck and held it there tightly.

Suddenly there was a flapping of wings and a *CAW-CAW* as a crow landed on the white fence at the front of the house, very close to Jemima.

'Oh no . . .' Amethyst whispered.

'What? What is it?' Ivy stuck her head out of the door to get a look, but Amethyst put her arm out and pushed her back. The crow looked from the faces huddled in the open doorway to Jemima, who had clocked the bird and taken a step backwards, her face curled up in disgust at it.

'What's going on, Amethyst?' Maggie asked.

'Ever wondered why this place is called Crowood Peak?' Amethyst kept her voice low so as not to scare Jemima or the other children, who were crowding closer and closer to them in the doorway. She raised her voice over the howling wind, which was whipping the few leaves left on the trees into a rustling frenzy. 'Jemima, you need to get inside right now!'

'Shoo!' Jemima hissed, but the bird simply hopped closer. 'I said, SHOO, you stupid bird!'

CAW! the bird replied in a menacing tone that made the hairs on Maggie and Ivy's necks stand on end.

'So, this place is called Crowood because there are lots of crows? So what?' Isaac asked, eavesdropping. 'I've always quite liked them.'

'That's not entirely the whole story.' Amethyst turned back to Jemima, not letting the crow out of her sight. 'They belong to *her*. She put them here to do her bidding and spy on everyone in the area, and that's exactly what they've been doing for years. Hundreds of little flying minions who report back to the Crowood Witch. No one can even so much as whisper near a crow without Emerald knowing about it.'

'And this crow in particular is also one of hers?' Ivy asked. 'It just looks like a normal –' Just then the bird twisted its head, and in the light of the street lamps they could clearly see its eyes glow green. 'Never mind. It's definitely one of hers. What do we do?' she whispered.

'Why is it looking at me like that?' Jemima's voice was beginning to tremble as the bird hopped closer and closer, cocking its head to the side and eyeing her with its beady glare. 'Get away from me, you filthy thing!' She batted her hands at it, but it stayed exactly where it was and was joined by a second crow. It landed on the other side of Jemima and fixed her with the same look in its eye.

'Jemima, you need to get inside now.'

'No. This is just some elaborate hoax and I won't fall for it.'

'Jemima, I promise you that no one is playing a trick on you.'

'No one except the witch!' Maggie scoffed.

'W-w-what?' Jemima stuttered, unable to take her eyes off the crows. 'They're only crows. Just . . . harmless . . . birds . . .' Suddenly Jemima was surrounded by more crows than any of them could count. They settled along the fence, on the pavement around her feet, on the grass in Amethyst's front garden, and, more importantly, all along the long path between them and Jemima. 'I'm going home now,' Jemima said with a firm nod, but her voice was wobbly. She took a step away from the gate, but a crow nipped at her bare ankle and the others cawed loudly. 'Stop that!' Jemima swatted the air around her knees, not daring to take an actual swipe at a bird, for fear of accidentally touching one of the creatures. She tried to take another step, but this time a crow nipped her so hard it broke the skin and drew blood.

'Amethyst, help her!' Maggie pleaded.

'My magic isn't strong enough. Whatever spell has a hold on these crows is far superior to anything I can conjure up.'

129

'You have to try, Amethyst! I know she's a bit of a pain but . . . she's still someone's daughter. Even if they've forgotten who she is,' Ivy begged. 'This murder of crows could *actually* murder Jemima!'

Amy nodded, but the dark circles under her eyes seemed to grow even darker at the mere thought of having to produce such powerful magic. She rubbed her hands together, shot a little silent prayer up to the moon and tried to stir her magic up from within.

'Magic is a very personal thing,' she explained. 'Some people have to think the happiest thoughts they can in order to summon their most powerful magic; some let their minds go blank and need perfect silence; and some, like the Crowood Witch, need to eat the hearts of pure and innocent children to perform their darkest spells.' She paused and looked a bit bashful. 'I myself need something a little different to conjure my most powerful magic for the bigger and more complicated spells. Promise me that . . . you won't laugh?'

Ivy and Maggie crossed their hearts and the other children did the same. None of them knew quite what to expect, but they certainly did not expect Amethyst to start singing.

'I wish I may, I wish I might,
But not on stars I see tonight.
Instead I'll wish upon the moon,
And hope she hears my hopeful tune.'

Maggie and Ivy exchanged looks with raised eyebrows.

'Singing?' Maggie whispered behind Amethyst's back, to which Ivy shrugged, both suddenly beginning to doubt the person they'd put their faith in.

'*SHHH!*' Amethyst hushed them with her eyes still closed. Her hands were beginning to glow, still not very bright, but much brighter than before.

'*Fiddle di dee and fiddle di doo,*
My heart is sweet, my heart is true.'

'It's a rather silly song, isn't it?' Ivy muttered.

'That is precisely why it works so well! Now, *shhh*!' Amethyst hissed out of the corner of her mouth as she continued her song:

'*Fiddle di doo and fiddle di dee,*
May the moon shine just for me.'

Amethyst shot her hand out in front of her towards Jemima. Her purple magic glittered through the air and created a shimmering bubble round the girl, who gasped loudly. Her eyes were wide in awe for a moment, but she quickly shook her head and her face returned to its usual scowl.

The crows cawed loudly and flapped their wings, hopping from foot to foot. One of them flew with all its might towards Jemima. Maggie and Ivy braced themselves for the moment it flew into Jemima's head, waiting for a shriek and a tangle of wings, claws and hair. Instead there was a comical *BOING!* noise as the bird bounced off the bubble round Jemima and was thrown over a metre into the air, before it flapped its wings and flew away.

'You're doing it, Amethyst!' Ivy cheered.

'Yes, but I need her to come back to us. My magic won't hold for long.' Amethyst's voice was strained, her hands beginning to shake.

'Jemima! Come here! The crows can't get you in the bubble! You'll be safe!' Ivy yelled down the pathway.

'I told you . . .' Jemima said, flinching as another crow threw itself at the force field, 'I'm going home.' She turned away from them, but paused before taking a step.

'Jemima, I can't protect you outside this house. We need to stay together!' Amethyst called.

'But . . . but . . . I want to go home.' For the first time, Jemima's angry, icy exterior cracked and everyone got a glimpse of the small child beneath. She was as scared as everyone else, as in need of her parents as the rest of them. So much so, that she was willing to risk her safety to get back to them, even though she knew they might not even know who she was.

'I'm going to get her,' Maggie said, and she stepped out of the doorway before anyone could stop her.

'Maggie, no!' Ivy tried to grab the back of her pyjamas but Maggie was too quick.

'If I'm fast enough, the witch won't know!' Maggie ran down the pathway, not caring how many crows she disturbed. She swung the gate open and reached into the force field, which happily let her arm through, to take hold of Jemima's wrist and drag her down the path towards the house.

Jemima was reluctant at first, trying to snatch her arm away and digging in her heels against each paving stone, but then Maggie felt her fingers clamp round hers and her feet begin to run in the same direction, as the crows started to hurtle at frightening speed at the bubble. As the crows flapped their wings, the green glitter of Emerald's magic poured off their feathers. It smelled like damp grass and burning wood fires. These crows were certainly Emerald's minions. Maggie's heart began to pound in her chest. The crows were bouncing off Jemima's force field but slamming directly into her – she could feel their beaks snapping at her dressing gown and their claws piercing the fabric.

'Amethyst, you have to make the force field bigger! Maggie's in danger!' Ivy cried.

'I . . . can't . . .' Amethyst said between strained, panting breaths. 'If I try . . . to make it bigger, it might collapse altogether . . . and then . . . we lose them both . . .!'

Ivy watched helplessly as the crows engulfed Maggie. Maggie could see Ivy and all the children in the house behind her, beckoning to her, and although Ivy's mouth was opening and closing, Maggie could only hear the sound of the birds squawking in her ears. Suddenly she could feel Jemima's hand tugging on hers – and then she felt their hands being slowly pulled apart. It was only then that Maggie realized her feet were no longer touching the ground!

An involuntary scream rose out of the deepest place in her chest. The crows had dug their claws into her socks, her dressing gown and her long purple hair, and were pulling her upwards. Several of the frightening feathered things had swarmed around her, creating a tornado-like orb that was sucking her off the ground and into the sky.

Jemima tried to hold on to Maggie for as long as she could, but when she felt her feet begin to lift off the ground too, she couldn't hold on any longer. She slipped down on to the pathway with a thump and watched as the crows created a glittering green mass around Maggie. Amethyst kept her magic surrounding Jemima, but as soon as the girl had cleared the doorway and was safely back inside the house, Amethyst let her magic spell break. The purple force field surrounding Jemima popped with the same satisfying noise that bubblegum makes when it bursts.

'MAGGIE!' Ivy yelled up to the night sky, but it was no use. Ivy could no longer even see Maggie through the sheer number of crows that were cawing and flapping violently near her. They flew higher and higher and further and further away, until the floating orb was only a glowing green dot against the night sky.

'I'm so sorry, Ivy . . . I'm so sorry . . .' Amethyst whispered. And then she fainted.

12
The Bond Between Friends

The hour that followed felt like an eternity to the children of Crowood Peak. Jemima tried to tell everyone how brave she'd been when the crows had come for her. She simply couldn't understand why no one seemed to be listening to her story of heroism, and so she huffed away to sulk in the corner.

Ivy made Isaac boil the kettle and make hot chocolate for everyone. She fetched a damp flannel, and when Eddie, Jennifer and Jamie had carried – well, dragged – Amethyst's limp body to the sofa, Ivy dabbed her forehead. Amethyst was cold to the touch so she got Jennifer to search the house for the warmest and cosiest blanket she could find so they could wrap Amethyst up nice and toasty until she woke. When her eyes finally fluttered open, they weren't anywhere near as purple as they had been. Instead of deep plum, they were now a faint lilac colour. Amethyst's magic was weak. Weaker than it had ever been.

'Maggie . . . Maggie! Where's Maggie?' Amethyst sat bolt upright abruptly, making everyone jump. She threw the blanket on to the sofa as she launched herself at the window.

'The crows took her,' Ivy said.

'They took her up to the top of the mountain,' Isaac explained.

'Where that mean old witch lady lives,' Darla said, while sucking her thumb.

'No thanks to you,' Jemima tutted.

'No thanks to *you*, you mean!' Ivy pointed an accusatory finger across the room to where Jemima had propped herself up against the wall, her arms folded. She looked lonely without Jennifer and Jamie standing behind her, nodding and agreeing with her every word. '*You* are the reason Amethyst is exhausted and weak and might not be able to protect us all. *You* are the reason Maggie left the house in the first place, because you wouldn't listen to us, and now my best friend is probably going to get her heart eaten by a wicked witch!' There was nothing but silence. None of the children in the house were looking at Ivy; instead they were looking at Jemima.

'Don't blame me for getting us into this mess. You two are always causing trouble. What is it you call yourselves – the Double Trouble Society? How stupid.'

Ivy had managed to stay strong while Amethyst had been unconscious. She wasn't by any means the oldest in the room, but she was the most knowledgeable about the situation and that had given her the courage to speak up. But now that Amethyst was awake and taking charge, Ivy felt that courage slip away from her like the magic that was draining from Amethyst. As hot and uncontrollable tears began to pour down her face, Ivy turned away from Jemima, who seemed unaffected by Ivy's accusations. She joined Amethyst at the window, who placed her hands on her shoulders and gently squeezed.

'It's all right, Ivy. We'll get Maggie back,' Amethyst whispered, resting her chin on the top of Ivy's head as they gazed up at the mountain. The smoke was thick and black and swirling like a terrifying tornado. Bolts of green lightning sizzled every few seconds and Ivy couldn't help but imagine Maggie lying lifeless at Emerald's feet, her heart missing from her chest.

'What if it's already too late?'

'Well, firstly, if I know my sister, she doesn't do things quietly. She'll make claiming the thirteenth child a real event. This is three hundred years in the making, so she'll want as many people watching as possible.' Ivy shivered under

Amethyst's hands at the mere thought of what the witch might do. 'And secondly,' Amethyst continued, 'you and Maggie are such good friends. The *best* of friends. You have a connection and a bond like sisters. If something had happened to her, you would have felt it by now. You would know.'

Ivy turned her head to Amethyst and raised an eyebrow. 'I . . . I would have felt it?'

'Listen to me.' Amethyst turned and crouched down to look into Ivy's blue eyes through her gold-rimmed glasses. 'I meant it when I said there's a little bit of magic in us all. Some people are born with a lot of magic. We call them witches. But *others* are born with a little bit of magic in them that stays with them always. This magic shows itself as "miracles" or "coincidences". Have you ever thought of someone right before the phone rings and then you pick it up and it turns out it's them? Have you ever become so engrossed in a book that you don't feel the hours slipping by? Have you ever had *déjà vu*? Or dreamed of something happening that then really happens? That, my dear girl, is *magic*.'

'And you think magic ties me and Maggie together?' Ivy asked hopefully.

'Oh, yes, Ivy. I do. Friends who find a deep connection right down to their very souls: I think that's magic. Friends who don't have to say anything to know what the other is thinking. Who can spend days apart and then pick up right where they left off the next time they see each other, as if not

a single second has passed. Friends who are more like family.'
Amethyst smiled and Ivy looked back out of the window,
fiddling with the end of her very purple plaits. 'I reckon if
you close your eyes and concentrate, you'll be able to feel
Maggie's energy.'

'How do I do that?' Ivy asked, already focusing her
attention towards the mountain, towards her best friend.

'Close your eyes and picture Maggie's face in your mind.
Now remember what it feels like when Maggie is standing
close to you.'

'She's usually pretty hyperactive. She can never simply
stand still and she often makes me feel dizzy.'

Amethyst laughed. 'Good! That's good. Now think of that
and try to *amplify* it. Make her energy as big and vibrant as
you can.'

Ivy's fingers began to tingle like they did when she'd been
lying on them in the night and had woken up with pins and
needles. Then her whole body began to feel warm like she
had got into a nice hot bath after being outside in the rain. 'I
think . . . I think I can feel her!' she murmured.

'Ivy . . .' Amethyst said, her voice quiet.

'I can see her in my mind more clearly now!'

'Ivy . . .' Amethyst croaked again.

'She looks like she's scared . . .' Ivy said, but then Amethyst
gently took her wrists, and when Ivy opened her eyes she
saw that her hands were glowing. 'What's happening to me?!'

Ivy asked, the glow beginning to fade now that she was no longer focused. 'That looks like your magic does, Amethyst – like when you were putting that force field round Jemima!'

'It does indeed.' Amethyst was astounded, unable to take her eyes off Ivy, staring at her hands and her hair. 'I wonder . . .'

'What?! What is it?!' Ivy asked, holding her hands out in front of her as though she was holding something rotten, her fingers trembling.

'No need to panic, Ivy – I just want to test something, OK?' Amethyst made her way through the children to her bookshelves and picked a book called *Hocus Pocus for Those Who Can't Focus*. 'I need you to concentrate very hard. Hands up in front of you, like you've seen me do. Now, deep breaths and repeat after me: *I wish I may, I wish I might* . . .' Amethyst began.

'I . . . I wish I may, I wish I might,' Ivy said, her voice shaking.

'*Create a spark of dazzling light!*'

Ivy repeated the end of the spell and a tiny little light about the size of a firefly appeared in front of her hands. The children gasped in awe. The light was small and weak, but it was there nonetheless. Ivy had conjured a spell! Ivy had *magic*.

'Well, would you look at that!' Amethyst snapped the book shut with a flourish that made Ivy jump so hard that the light extinguished itself with a little *pop!* The watching children cheered and applauded, all except Jemima, who rolled her eyes.

'How . . . how am I able to do that? I've never been able to do that before! Ever! Not even by accident!' Ivy said with a small smile.

'I think the reason my magic is so weak and your hair is so very purple is because, when I hit you with that spell, I gave some of my magic to you and Maggie.'

'But why is her hair getting brighter?' Jemima piped up from her corner.

'My guess would be that Ivy and Maggie have such a strong bond between them that the magic of their friendship is mingling with my magic and getting stronger,' Amethyst said. She turned back to Ivy. 'The fact that you two must miss each other so much right now means your magic is being tested. Clearly, it's proving its strength – your hair is quite alarming to look at now!' She laughed and Ivy scowled, but then caught sight of her reflection in the window.

'Oh, wow. Yeah, OK. I agree with Jemima. This really isn't a good look,' Ivy said, giggling.

'Well, this is quite a turn-up for the books! We can use this to our advantage.' Amethyst rubbed her hands together and then guided Ivy back to the window.

'We can?'

'We can indeed. I need you to do again what you did before. Think of Maggie and her energy, but this time I need you to focus on her voice. Think of what she sounds like and how hearing her voice makes you feel. Then, if she's saying something right now . . . you might be able to hear her and we'll know if she's safe.'

Ivy looked towards the mountain once more and closed her eyes. She thought of Maggie's bright energy, her warm smile, her long black hair swinging wildly around her – Maggie always tended to bounce or run wherever she went. Then she thought of her voice. Loud and confident. Never wavering, but always kind. And then Ivy heard it as clear as a bell in her mind. It was Maggie's voice and there was no mistaking it.

'*Don't worry, Ivy. We'll defeat this wicked witch somehow.*'

13
Taking Flight

All of a sudden the crows stopped their flapping, flew through an opening and dropped Maggie several metres down on to the ground with a loud thud. Maggie, muttering about squished biscuits and being covered in bruises, got to her feet to look around. She was in a stone cave where a small green fire burned in the darkness. Its green light softly illuminated the walls of the cave, but Maggie noticed another light bouncing off them too. Something warmer and more purple. It was only when a strand of hair flopped into her eyes that she realized it was her purple hair glowing wildly in the dark.

'Cool!' she said with a grin. It was blindingly bright, so she brushed it out of her face and moved forward, using it to light her way as she looked for a way out. The chill of the air set into her bones quickly, however, and her teeth chattered with fear and cold as she followed the sound of the gusty wind outside. It stirred her purple hair into a wild dance, and the closer she fumbled in the dark towards what she hoped was the opening of the cave, the louder the noise grew. It was a cackling that echoed around the stone walls and made her skin prickle and the hairs on her arms and neck stand on end. Each step she took was more nervous than the last, her legs wobbly and her knees knocking together.

Then she saw her: the Crowood Witch, up close and in the flesh. Emerald had her back to Maggie. She was still in the same black fur dress she had worn after her transition from her cat body, and her long black hair twisted through the air like snakes snapping at their prey. The witch waved her arms around her head, her bony fingers glowing green, and every few moments she shot sparks up to the sky that exploded into the smoke like fireworks. The smell of dead grass and rotting leaves got stronger with each explosion and the witch's laugh grew louder and more maniacal.

Maggie crept out of the cave and walked over to the edge of the mountain. The drop made her stomach turn, but she looked down at the village below, smaller than she'd ever seen it, and thought of Ivy and how scared she must be.

'Don't worry, Ivy. We'll defeat this wicked witch somehow,' she muttered to herself. Then, abruptly, the cackling ceased. The witch whipped her head round and glared at Maggie with her shining black eyes. Her skin was so very pale, just like Amethyst's, but her lips were thin and her face was sharp and unkind, although still fascinating in an unnerving and deeply unapproachable way.

'Wicked? Did you just call me *wicked*?' the witch hissed. Maggie thought her voice sounded like a cat when it spat. 'Yes, I suppose that's a good way to describe me. I'm glad you're here, Maggie, dear. I actually wanted to thank you.'

'Th-th-thank me?' Maggie's bottom lip began to wobble, but she bit her cheeks to keep from crying in front of the witch.

'Yes,' the witch purred. 'You broke the dozen's circle. You told me the spell was broken. If it wasn't for you, I'd still be trapped as a cat, completely powerless. You are responsible for the despair and destruction I'm about to rain down upon the world – the most vicious storm you poor little humans have ever seen.'

'That's not true.' Maggie felt a tear slide down her cheek and she quickly wiped it away. 'This isn't *my* fault.'

'Children are *always* to blame,' Emerald snapped. 'Every single one of the little nuisances. That's why I plan to get rid of you all.' She licked the back of her hand and smoothed down her hair with it.

'W-w-what?' Maggie stuttered.

'Oh, yes! Do you really think I would stop at just the thirteenth? Why on earth would I do that when I could eat the heart of every child in the entire world and live until the end of time?' A screech of triumph burst out of the witch. She raised her palms to the swirling smoke cloud above them and green lightning crackled, showering sparks down around them that singed Maggie's purple hair. 'All right. Maybe *all* the hearts in the world might be a little much for me. My servants – the adults I choose to take with me – will do my bidding. Eat a heart each so that they can be by my side for longer. I'm sure your father, for instance, wouldn't mind adding a few more years to his life, would he not?'

'My father would never eat the heart of a child!' Maggie felt anger build inside her. How dare the witch speak of her father like that! 'My father is a good man!' Maggie could feel the rage bubbling in her stomach like a potion in a storybook cauldron.

'*Your father* . . .' the witch hissed with eyes as black as coal, 'will do whatever I tell him to.' Her thin lips turned up at the corners into something Maggie wasn't able to call a smile. Smiles are meant to make you feel warm and loved, but Emerald's smile made Maggie shudder and feel very, very afraid. 'He's under a spell so deep and so dark it'll be a wonder if he ever wakes from it. If I tell him to eat a heart, he *will* eat one! Even if it is yours, or your friend's! I must say, I have really outdone myself this time.' Emerald turned her eyes towards the sky and looked up at the enormous cloud of smoke that glistened green in the light of the moon. 'There isn't a single witch alive who could counter this spell. I'm afraid you and your little playmates are doomed.' The witch began to shake with laughter. She bent double and screeched and howled, her hands beginning to glow green again and shoot sparks upwards into the smoke.

'You *won't* get away with this!' Maggie yelled. 'Amethyst will find a way to stop you! She did last time and she will this time too! She's a thousand times the witch you'll ever be!' But Emerald didn't hear her over her own shrill laughter and the sound of her evil magic shooting upwards like exploding fireworks.

Maggie could feel the rage in her stomach spread through her body like wildfire. It was hot and potent, and suddenly she stamped her foot against the rock of the mountain as hard as she could. A purple bolt of lightning shot from the sole of her slipper, burning the bottom of it clean off. The bolt of lightning cracked the rock at her feet, then ran all the way from her to the bare, clawed feet of the evil witch. Emerald yelped and hopped backwards as the lightning burned the ends of her toes. Then her expression changed from wicked delight to pure and unbridled malice.

'Maggie has magic, eh? My sister up to her usual tricks, hmm? Well, let's see how well she's taught you then, shall we?' The witch raised her glowing hands in front of her, ready to blast Maggie with a spell to send her hurtling off the mountain, but a low rumbling sound made her stop in her tracks. Suddenly the sound became deafening and Maggie's heart plummeted to the bottom of the mountain. Was she going to end up there at any moment? The lightning bolt had separated the chunk of rock she was standing on from the rest of the mountain, and that chunk was now crumbling away and taking Maggie with it. The witch laughed and waved goodbye as Maggie began to tumble towards the ground below . . .

Maggie let out a scream of terror as she continued to fall. 'HELP!' she shrieked, and clenched her eyes tight. Fear shot through her body, like the anger she had felt just before creating the lightning bolt, but then she felt a warm feeling suddenly rush through her veins. The glow reached her fingertips and her toes and the top of her head. Suddenly she realized the wind was no longer rushing towards her and she was no longer falling towards the ground. When she opened her eyes, she realized that she was actually moving upwards, and away from her untimely death. She was flying! Her whole body was aglow with a purple hue, and as triumph flushed through her, the glow got even brighter. Maggie rose through the air and back up to the witch, who looked ever so displeased to see her.

'How have you done this?!' Emerald howled.

This time it was Maggie's turn to laugh. She poked her tongue out at the witch, and before Emerald could respond with a spell that would turn her into a toad, Maggie flew away as fast as she could. Amethyst's magic had drained away when the crows had taken Maggie, but it was back now. Maggie was *flying*. It was something she'd only ever been able to do in dreams, and who knew how long it might last. She was wobbly at first, but soon enough she was swirling through the air like she'd been born with wings.

'*YAAAAAAHHHHHOOOOOOO!!!!!*' Maggie yelled into the sky, and she thought of Peter Pan shooting through the air, leaving a trail of pixie dust behind him. But she didn't need pixie dust. The magic was rushing through her veins. This was the closest Maggie had ever been to the stars, and seeing them shine that little bit brighter sent tingles up her whole body. She tried a loop-the-loop, which was a little lopsided, but she still giggled the whole way round. The village looked miniature below – the parked cars the size of ants – and Maggie didn't want her feet to touch the ground again. Flying made her feel free and alive, and as if no worry or problem could ever be that bad – not from these dizzying heights. She let out a burst of laughter, and with it a burst of purple light lit up the sky around her.

She may have figured out the flying and worked out how to navigate her way home, but landing was proving tricky. After a few failed attempts, she finally hit the grass with a less-than-graceful thud, adding a few more bruises to her collection. This wouldn't have been embarrassing had Amethyst, Ivy and all the children of Crowood Peak not been out on the front lawn of Hokum House waiting for her. They cheered and clapped as she thumped to the ground. She suddenly felt exhausted, and Ivy ran to her with open arms.

'I'm so glad you're OK!' Ivy yelled in Maggie's ear, hugging her so tightly she almost knocked the breath out of her. 'I really thought the witch was going to burn you to a cinder with a single blast of her magic! But you really showed her! *You won't get away with this!*' Ivy mimicked the words Maggie had spoken to the witch on the mountain. She was out of breath from the excitement of it all.

'How do you know that's what I said?' Maggie croaked as Ivy finally let her go.

'Let's just say we won't be needing our walkie-talkies any more!' Ivy said, and then laughed even harder when Maggie's face scrunched up in confusion. Ivy concentrated as hard as she could on pushing her thoughts into Maggie's mind. Without speaking out loud, Ivy said, *Come in, Maggie. I repeat, come in, Maggie. Over.*

Maggie's eyes grew wide and round as she heard Ivy's voice loud and clear in her own head, without seeing her lips moving. 'Whoa!' she said in amazement. 'How did you do that?! Teach me!'

'Only if you teach me to fly!' Ivy exclaimed.

'Did you know our hair glows in the dark too?' Maggie said.

'What?! I knew it was bright, but it's actually phosphorescent?!'

'Yeah, it's . . . it's fossil-crescent!' Maggie agreed, and Ivy laughed.

'No, *phos-phor-es-cent*. It means glows in the dark!'

'OK, you two. There will be time for this later, but right now we have bigger fish to fry. Or rather, a bigger witch to defeat.' Amethyst pointed towards the mountain, where Emerald was putting on a very frightening and extremely smoky light show of spells.

'Wow. You must have really annoyed her,' Ivy said.

'Yeah, she definitely did not expect me to fly. The look on her face would have been funny if it wasn't so terrifying. So, you heard everything the witch was saying too?'

'Sort of. I could only hear what was in your head, so your words were louder than hers, but . . . we got the gist,' Ivy said sadly.

'Emerald plans to erase children by putting a spell on every adult on Earth. The adults will live forever, by eating the hearts of children, and every child will be wiped out for good,' Maggie explained to everyone, trying to keep the wobble out of her voice.

'No!' Eddie gasped. 'My mum wouldn't, couldn't –'

'You've got to be wrong!' Jamie said, sounding frightened. 'My dad would never –'

'Well, *I* believe you. So what do we do?' Isaac asked with a tremble in his voice. He was still clutching his jar of gunk.

'Yeah, what's the plan?' asked Jennifer.

'They don't have one,' Jemima scoffed from the doorway of Hokum House, reluctant to get close enough in case she seemed like part of the team. 'They're making it up as they go along.'

'Yes, we are,' Amethyst confirmed. 'I'm not pretending to have this figured out. If I've given anyone the impression I know what I'm doing, then I'm truly sorry, because I don't.' Amethyst spoke to everyone as a group, trying hard not to acknowledge Jemima's negative attitude. 'But that doesn't mean we won't figure this out together or that my sister won't be defeated. I believe we can do this, but not if we don't all believe we can, or if we aren't willing to try.'

The group nodded and made agreeing noises, but Jemima just rolled her eyes. She didn't complain, though, and Amethyst took that as a small win.

'Right, everyone. It's late. Let's try to get some sleep because I fear tomorrow might bring with it new horrors we can't even imagine.' Amethyst sighed and ushered everyone back inside the house, except for Maggie and Ivy. 'Just a minute, you two.'

Maggie was mid-yawn, her mouth stretching open as wide as it could go, and Ivy blinked slowly, already feeling sleep begin to creep over her.

'I need your help. This house is without any protection, and although I don't think Emerald will attack tonight, I still think it would be wise to put some spells in place.'

'We don't know how to do any protection spells, Amethyst,' Ivy said, catching Maggie's yawn.

'No, but I do. I need you to boost my magic. Take my hands.' Maggie and Ivy stood either side of Amethyst and sleepily took her hands. 'Now, I need you to imagine how you would feel if someone was trying to hurt anyone you love.'

'I don't want to think about that,' Maggie said.

'I need you to. But only for a moment, because then I need you to imagine yourself protecting them. Imagine how it feels to be strong and brave enough to stop something from hurting the people or the things you love the most. Imagine feeling unstoppable, invincible even. Let that feeling fill you up and then let it spill over and across this house and everyone inside it. That kind of love is real magic. It's what keeps people safe.' Amethyst held on to their hands as tightly as she could and they both squeezed back.

'Even Jemima?' Ivy said huffily.

'Even Jemima.' Amethyst nodded, with a small smile.

'Fine.' Ivy sighed, and then closed her eyes to concentrate. Together Ivy and Maggie imagined themselves as a united force. They imagined the witch coming to turn their dads into heart-eating monsters, but they also imagined themselves as capable of stopping her. They imagined themselves being filled with powerful good magic, strong enough to blast the wicked witch out of existence and back to the demon her aunt had bargained with three hundred years ago. Then they pictured themselves as the saviours of Crowood Peak, and the village holding a festival to celebrate their victory forever more. As they imagined this, a purple light shone out from their hearts and shimmered across the entire house, wrapping it up in a warm hug that would keep everyone safe and sound for at least one more night.

As they went back inside, the milky-white moon above them shone down on the house.

Tomorrow, it would be a blue moon.

14
Golden Words

'*Three hundred years she won't be seen . . .* This is obvious. She was defeated by Amethyst three hundred years ago and hadn't been seen – except as a cat – until her return the other day,' Ivy explained as they sat around eating their breakfast. Amethyst's magic was stronger now that she had rested, but it still wasn't as strong as the magic she'd accidentally given Maggie and Ivy, so she'd quickly taught them some simple spells, like how to brew tea, boil eggs, make rounds and rounds of toast, and squeeze orange juice, with and without bits. Oranges whizzed through the air, knives delicately sliced through them when they reached the chopping board, and then the two halves squeezed themselves into a big pitcher, which then poured the fresh juice into everyone's glasses round the kitchen table.

They even conjured up several different types of jam. Maggie and Ivy hadn't known how to make jam, but Amethyst taught them a simple multiplying spell. They took jam jars from Amethyst's cupboard that were half full and multiplied the contents until the jars were full to the brim with delicious raspberry, strawberry and blackberry jam. Everyone was delighted. Even Jemima's eyes widened with glee at the spread set out before them, although she didn't manage to produce a thank you.

Maggie and Ivy had slept soundly through the night despite the worries on their minds. They figured the flying and mind-reading had worn them out. However, now they were awake, the only thing they could think about was defeating the witch once and for all.

'*But she'll return to claim thirteen* . . . again, obvious. She's returned not only to claim the thirteenth child to seal her deal with the demon, but she's also worked out a way to extend that deal to every grown-up in the world,' Maggie said, and Ivy gulped at the thought.

'*The sky will crack, the earth will shake, when the dozen's circle breaks* . . .'

'That bit is no thanks to you two,' Jemima said, stuffing a slice of toast into her mouth.

157

'Yes, all right, we feel bad enough as it is, thank you,' Maggie said, sliding the toast rack away from Jemima just as she was reaching for another piece. 'You'd think she'd be nicer to us knowing we have the power to turn her into a pile of maggots,' Maggie whispered, and Ivy almost choked on her juice.

'*But when the thirteenth moon is blue, two sisters, fierce and brave and true, will send the witch to death's embrace, and to her final resting place,*' Amethyst stated, finishing the prophecy for them, and everyone fell silent.

'OK. So when is the next blue moon?' Maggie asked, spreading a mountain of blackberry jam on to a piece of thick white bread.

'A blue moon isn't actually a moon that's blue,' said a voice from down the far end of the table. It came from behind one of Amethyst's spell books, a big leathery tome with gold-embossed writing that said: *Phases of the Moon for Buffoons.* Crystals jutted out from the leather in a circle round the title and glinted in the light. Eddie lifted his head above the book so that they could see his eyes. 'Just thought that might be of interest.'

'He's right,' Ivy said. 'Usually, we only have twelve full moons in a year, but around every two and a half years we have thirteen. That thirteenth full moon – the third out of four in three months – is what we call a blue moon.' Eddie looked up and gave Ivy the faintest hint of a smile before putting his nose back in the book. Ivy felt her face flush for the briefest moment but managed to disguise it behind her glass of orange juice.

'So . . . the saying "once in a blue moon" actually means "about once in two and a half years"?' Maggie asked.

'Technically, yes,' Ivy confirmed.

'OK. We've got the festival tonight, celebrating when the witch was defeated – I'm meant to be reading out one of the names! – but it's not always on the exact day of the blue moon, is it?'

'It should be,' Ivy said. 'But grown-ups always pick the nearest Friday or Saturday to start so it can go on all weekend.'

'It's tonight.' Amethyst slapped a copy of the daily newspaper down on the table in between their crumb-strewn plates. The headline read:

FESTIVAL FOR THE TWELVE BEGINS TONIGHT!

Maggie picked up the newspaper and flipped to the page where her dad's story usually was, but instead it showed an advert for a toffee-apple stall that would be opening that evening. Maggie's heart sank at the thought of her dad being alone in their home, probably confused by all her things that were strewn around. She wondered what he must be thinking and feeling, and sent a little thought up into the air and over to him, although he probably had no idea who she was.

'So, we only have until the full moon tonight to come up with a plan to defeat a three-hundred-year-old witch? Led by her sister who can't even magic up breakfast? It was nice knowing you all.' Jemima laughed haughtily.

'That is IT!' Maggie stood up so quickly her chair fell over behind her and hit the kitchen tiles with a whack. 'I have had enough of you and your negativity, once and for all. Let's see what this magic can really do, shall we?'

'Maggie, no!' Amethyst yelped, but Ivy got there first and jumped in front of Maggie's raised hands.

'Magic shouldn't be used for evil.'

'Evil? Turning Jemima into the little snake she is would be a public service! I don't think there's a single person here who wouldn't be thrilled to have a little less of her attitude.'

'I know and I agree,' Ivy said, 'but Amethyst has trusted us with this magic and I don't think she'd be too pleased to see us use it for something like this. Plus, neither of us knows how to do magic like that, and if it went horribly wrong and something happened to Jemima, you'd feel terrible. I know you would.'

Maggie leaned around Ivy and glared at Jemima. She looked suitably nervous, which Maggie decided was satisfaction enough. 'Fine,' Maggie agreed, and everyone in the room breathed a sigh of relief. 'But next time . . .'

'Next time, you can do what you like. But if Jemima knows what's good for her, there won't be a next time.'

Jemima couldn't shut up. 'There won't be a next time, because you both think you're talented witches but you're hopeless. The magician at my sixth birthday party was better than you three put together,' she scoffed.

Maggie turned a dangerous shade of tomato red, but before she could get any ideas about casting a spell herself, Amethyst grabbed an empty jam jar from the table and clicked her fingers. The sound was as loud as a firecracker. The lights in the kitchen began to flicker, but everyone was looking at Jemima. A red glow was travelling up her throat, and, as it came out of her open mouth, everyone could see what looked like glowing words. Jemima's words. Words like 'creepy', 'rubbish' and 'hopeless' jumped out. Some words were gold, like 'please' and 'thank you', but there were very few of those. As Amethyst held out the jar, the words drifted towards it.

'No need to be alarmed, everyone. I just think it'd be better if we had twenty-four hours of peace and quiet. This jar is slowly filling up with the words Jemima was going to say over the next day. Judging by how red the jar is, I think this spell can only be a good thing. Negativity like this will only slow us down!'

When the last red word had slid into the jar, Amethyst slammed the lid on and twisted it shut, and the kitchen lights stopped flickering.

Jemima scowled and opened her mouth to speak but nothing came out. She clutched her throat and it looked like she was attempting to scream by the way her face contorted and turned purple, but no one could hear a thing.

'When you've learned how to use your words responsibly and talk to people with kindness, you can have this back. But, until then, silence is golden. Unlike most of your words!' Amethyst held up the jar and swirled it gently like Maggie and Ivy had seen grown-ups do with glasses of wine. Slowly the golden words swirled into the others and the jar started to look like it contained shimmering sunbeams. There was not a single glimpse of red anywhere to be seen. Amethyst tucked the glass jar away into one of the deep pockets of her purple velvet coat and smiled. 'That's better.'

15
Flying

'Now,' Amethyst said, 'the blue moon is tonight and we need a plan. All the grown-ups in Crowood Peak will be preparing for the festival, which makes it a bit harder for us.'

'Why?' asked Maggie.

'Well, I told Max and Bill that you and Ivy were my nieces visiting from far away. If I said that about all of you, that would mean I have about fifty brothers and sisters!'

'Perhaps you run a summer school?' Ivy suggested.

'It isn't summer,' Eddie said, still staring into his book.

'Then an autumn school?' Maggie offered.

'There's no such thing,' Eddie said, sounding tired of their suggestions.

'Well, what's your idea then, if you're so clever?' Maggie said with her hands on her hips.

'How about an orphanage?' Eddie said as he glanced up from his book. An icy chill seemed to still the room. No one wanted to think about the possibility that their parents might never remember them. Where would that leave them?

'I think a school is a great idea, Ivy. This is a school for gifted students who have excelled in different areas and have been sent to me for tutoring.' Amethyst was trying her best to warm the children's spirits and distract them, but they remained quiet and looked downcast. 'Children, I know this is bleak. Maybe the bleakest situation you have found yourselves in so far. But I promise you we will do everything we can to try and defeat the witch. As long as we stick together we will find a way through this, no matter what.'

Jemima opened her mouth, having momentarily forgotten she had no voice to make any more quips.

'OK, *class*,' Amethyst said, with a pointed smile at Ivy and Maggie, 'let's put our heads together. Tell me all about this festival. Let's leave no stone unturned.'

'Well,' Maggie began, 'there are toffee apples, cookies and honeycomb covered in chocolate. There are also these biscuits . . . oh, the biscuits . . .' she whispered, momentarily lost in thought.

'Very helpful, Maggie, but . . . anything you can tell me that isn't about food?' Amethyst squeezed Maggie's shoulder and gave her a reassuring smile.

'We light candles and put them in our windows to guide the souls of the taken children back home to Crowood Peak,' said Issac. 'The people who now live in the houses those twelve children once lived in make their homes brighter than everyone else's by putting lanterns in the garden or stringing fairy lights round the front door.'

'Everyone wears emerald green, the colour of the first Arcturus witch's hair before it turned black, in the hope that the curse can be lifted and she can return to the person she was before,' explained Jennifer.

Amethyst shook her head, her mouth hanging open, unable to believe that the tragedy had sparked such a tradition.

'All the parents in the village recite the names of their own children to prove that they haven't . . . been forgotten . . .' Ivy's voice faded away as she realized that the parents wouldn't be able to recreate that particular tradition this year.

'So our parents are going to be asked to recite the names of their children, and not one parent is going to have a thing to say. Won't anyone think that's weird?' Isaac asked.

'I'm sure Emerald has found a way to wipe that particular tradition from everyone's minds,' Amethyst said, sighing.

'Don't forget the stones!' Maggie added. This was her favourite part. 'The twelve round this house.' She gulped. 'Including the one we moved.'

'We stand in a circle round the house, and twelve children from Crowood Peak read out the names of the lost children to honour their memory,' Ivy explained.

'And there's the salt!' Darla said.

'The salt, darling? What salt?' Amethyst hoisted little Darla and her unicorn up on to her lap and Darla gave a gleeful giggle.

'She means the salt we use to draw a circle round this house,' Ivy said.

'Why on earth would you do that?' Amethyst asked, laughing.

'To make sure no evil gets out?' Maggie said, as if that were not only an obvious answer but an answer a witch should most certainly know.

'But . . . that's not what salt circles are for. You're meant to draw a circle of salt round something in order to protect it. So that nothing evil gets *in*.'

'Are you telling me that all these years we've been protecting the Crowood Witch from anything evil getting to her?' Ivy let her head fall into her hands with a slap. 'The salt circle was pointless, then?'

'Not entirely,' Amethyst said. 'You protected my sister from any demons who might have wanted to free her from her feline form. All this chaos would have happened long before I got here to help if you hadn't been drawing salt circles round the house every blue moon. Does that make you feel any better?'

Ivy nodded. 'It does, actually.'

'Anyway, a salt circle might not be a bad idea for us tonight.'

'A bit of salt? Is that really enough to stop an evil witch?' Jennifer asked, reaching up on her tiptoes and opening the cupboards to find some salt. She found a red canister that had SALT on it in big white writing and threw it over to Amethyst.

Amethyst placed the salt on the table. 'Thank you. And yes, it'll take a lot more than a salt circle.' She sighed. 'But I don't believe my sister is entirely evil. Not yet, anyway.'

'Whoa, whoa, whoa – hang on a second. You're telling me that this is your sister when she *isn't* entirely evil?!' Maggie gasped, pointing furiously out of the window to the mountain. 'She can get worse than this?'

'I'm afraid so. She won't be entirely evil until her deal with the demon is complete. Until then, there is a tiny little bit of good left in her heart.'

'That's incredibly hard to believe,' Eddie said drily from behind his book. 'But maybe that's the key to this.'

A warm silence filled the air of the kitchen. 'What do you mean?' Amethyst asked slowly, not wanting to scare away this newly forming idea.

'Look here.' Eddie thumped a book down on the table entitled *Buds for Duds*. 'I've been reading about a certain kind of flower that is almost impossible to destroy.'

'You're not filling me with confidence here, Eddie.' Maggie put her elbow on his shoulder and leaned in to look at the page he'd opened. There was a diagram of a wilted, almost-dead flower.

'I'm not saying the witch will be impossible to kill.' He rolled his eyes impatiently. 'If you'd let me finish, I was going to say that this flower is so hard to kill because, if there is even a tiny bit of life left inside, it will cling on to that life until someone comes along and gives it water and sunlight and helps it thrive. It could be withered and brown without a petal or green leaf in sight, but as long as there's still a little scrap of vitality left in it, you can bring it back from the brink of death.' Eddie looked up, expecting everyone to be beaming at him with joy.

'. . . So?' Maggie finally broke the silence.

Eddie sighed. 'What if it's the same with your sister, Amethyst? *If* you're right and there *is* still a tiny little sliver of goodness in the heart of the Crowood Witch, maybe there's a way to access it. To draw it out of her and make it grow. To bring her back from the brink of darkness.' Eddie shrugged, his eyes moving from left to right across the pages, still reading as he spoke. He seemed to have an old soul – it was as if he was a very wise eighty-year-old who had seen the entire

168

world and read thousands of books, trapped inside the body of a twelve-year-old.

'But how? There's so much darkness in there. How do we draw out that chink of light?' Ivy asked.

Eddie closed the book, then looked directly at Ivy, which made her cheeks feel hot. 'You find the things that make her happy or that used to make her happy.'

'My sister is only happy when she's inflicting pain,' Amethyst said.

'Is there nothing from your time together as children that you shared an interest in? Something that made you both equally as happy as each other?'

Amethyst was quiet for a moment. And then another. Until she was lost in thought entirely. She had very few good memories of her sister, but the ones she did have were all of the same thing – *flying*. She could practically feel the wind rushing through every strand of her hair, the warmth of her sister's body as she held on tightly with her arms round Emerald's waist, her cheek pressed against the space between her shoulder blades, and she could almost hear Emerald's sharp laugh ring out into the night – a real laugh, not a cackle. Filled with joy instead of malice. In that moment she knew what would draw out the goodness in Emerald's heart.

'Flying,' she finally said, returning her gaze to the room. 'We used to fly broomsticks. Emerald was always headstrong and unruly and full of her own opinions, and would fight with our parents. After every fight they had, she'd take my hand, hoist me on to the back of her broom and off we'd go – far higher than we could fly just on our own, and much further too. It was like leaving the world and all our cares behind. Everything melted away above the clouds. It was just us up there, together, and that was what mattered.'

The children listened to Amethyst, and as she spoke it was as if they were on broomsticks with her and Emerald.

'When we touched down on solid ground again, she wouldn't say much. She'd simply look at me and smile, and I had this warm feeling right in the centre of my chest – we were twin sisters and we would always be twin sisters, no matter what tried to come between us. But then . . . she fell under the spell of the curse and ran away.' Amethyst wiped away a tear and gave a little titter of embarrassment. 'I don't know if she still feels the same about flying now. Or about me, for that matter. After all, I'm the one who turned her into a cat and locked her in this house for three hundred years – she's sure to feel resentful. I doubt she's my biggest fan.'

'It's worth a try, isn't it?' Ivy begged.

'But what exactly is the plan here? How do we get her flying? And if we do get her on a broomstick, how do we know she'll enjoy it like she used to?' Maggie asked.

'How did you feel when you were flying, Maggie?' Amethyst asked, her lips turning up at the corners, already knowing Maggie's answer.

Maggie thought back to when she had been swirling through the air, and how even though there had been an evil witch zooming after her with a knife and fork ready to feast on her heart, it didn't matter because flying had felt so wonderful. 'Yeah, OK, fair point. And I haven't even tried a broomstick yet . . .' She nodded at Ivy. 'It'll *definitely* work.'

'But we've already seen her flying. She flew to the mountain, remember?' Jamie pointed out.

'I think I need to be *with* her,' Amethyst said, trying to keep the nervous wobble out of her voice. 'I'll need to get her on a broomstick with me so I can recreate those long, high flights we used to take as sisters. Hopefully that should jog her memory.'

'Isn't that super dangerous?' Isaac asked.

'Hmm – high in the air with an evil witch with far more magic than I can dream of? Yes, I'd say that fits into the category of super dangerous.' Amethyst laughed a little hysterically. 'But we have no other choice. I don't know how else we can make my sister see sense or reason unless I make her remember what life was like before she became this black-hearted monster. We were close before the curse took hold. Best friends, actually. I was always on her side, even when the curse first hit her and her hair turned from green to black. Then, one day, I woke up and she had gone.' Another tear escaped down Amethyst's cheek but she didn't wipe it away. She had disappeared again into her mind's eye.

'I sent her thoughts that I knew she could hear, but she never sent anything back. But as time went by, I began to feel drawn to Hokum House – its magic was calling to me – and I knew it must have meant she had returned here and woken up its magic to fulfil the prophecy of the Crowood Witch. So I came here and found her – but not as I had known her. She was no longer my sister. She was . . . something else.'

'Why did she come to Hokum House?' Maggie asked.

Amethyst shrugged. 'Curses have strange powers. They attach themselves to things that aren't always what was intended. The original curse was put on the first Arcturus witch in this house, and here the twelve children were taken, and so, when the curse passed on to Emerald, it called her back here – back to take the thirteenth child at the time of the next blue moon.'

'Oh good, I'm so glad we're here then . . .' Maggie mumbled.

'*Two sisters, fierce and brave and true* . . .' Ivy muttered.

'What?' Maggie nudged her with her elbow.

'The prophecy says that "*two sisters, fierce and brave and true*" will be able to defeat the witch. That's you and Emerald! Together you'll be able to defeat the darkness within her – the darkness from the original Crowood Witch – and stop her from becoming entirely evil!' Ivy clapped her hands together, not only extremely excited about the prospect of everything finally being over, but also very pleased that she'd been able to figure it out.

'I hope you're right, Ivy.' Amethyst rose to her feet, took a long, deep breath and said, 'Now, first things first. I'm going to need a broomstick.'

16

Jemima Can Talk

They made their way into the living room. Ivy took her notebook from her rucksack, opened it to a clean page and placed it on the coffee table, her pen in hand, ready to formulate a plan.

'A broomstick? Don't you already have one?' Maggie asked.

'I used to, but I don't fly much any more. Flying draws more attention than I'd like, so I sold mine and bought a cauldron instead. Much more suited to potions, me. I prefer walking or taking the train. I like the scenic route,' Amethyst said with a shy smile.

'How come Emerald doesn't need a broom? She flew up to that mountain by herself! And Maggie flew too. Can't you do the same thing?' Jamie asked, with a hint of Jemima's tone.

Amethyst very calmly stood up from her seat and gave a polite little cough into her hand to get everyone's attention. Her whole body began to give that purple glow and, at first, no one seemed to realize what was happening, but suddenly her head was almost touching the ceiling.

'Any witch worth her salt can fly without a broom. But you wouldn't walk all the way from here to London, would you? You'd be completely and utterly exhausted, wouldn't you?' She looked at Maggie. 'I expect you were very tired last night, right?' Maggie nodded. She had felt totally wiped out when she had gone to bed. 'No. For longer distances,' Amethyst continued, 'you hop on the train or take a car so you have somewhere to sit, and something else is doing the legwork. That, my friends, is the difference between flying with and without a broom.' Amethyst slowly made her way down from the ceiling and everyone gave her a round of applause.

'That was wicked, Amethyst!' Jamie cheered, and Jennifer clapped so fiercely and so fast that Amethyst was worried her hands might fall off. Jemima simply gave a little soundless sigh and went back to inspecting her fingernails in the corner.

'Thank you.' Amethyst flushed at their reaction, but straightened out her cloak and gave a little shake of her head to signal it was time to get back to business. 'Besides, it has to be a broomstick because that's how Emerald and I used to fly as children, high into the clouds. Every detail has to be as similar as possible to make her feel the same as she used to. She needs to remember that feeling of being free and happy and . . . and loved by her sister.' Amethyst lowered her head.

Ivy and Maggie shared a look. 'I hadn't really thought about how difficult this is for Amethyst. All we've talked about since she arrived is defeating her sister, which might mean . . . killing her,' Ivy whispered to Maggie.

'It'd be like if you turned evil and I had to kill you,' Maggie said. 'I don't think I could do it.'

'Why would I be the one to turn evil?' Ivy said, aghast.

'I'm just saying! You wouldn't be able to kill *me* if I turned green and wicked! Right?'

'I dunno. I reckon I'd manage somehow,' Ivy said teasingly.

'Yeah, right. I saw your face as those crows carried me away. You were distraught. Practically beside yourself. Absolutely racked with fear!' Maggie said dramatically, and Ivy couldn't help but giggle.

'Yeah, all right, I was pretty worried,' Ivy admitted. 'You were fine, though, so stop milking it.'

'Fair enough,' Maggie said, laughing.

'Everything OK, you two?' Amethyst asked.

'Fine.' They giggled. 'What sort of thing are we looking for then? For your broom?'

'Yeah – will anything do? My dad's a gardener so I'm pretty sure there's one in our garage!' Isaac offered.

'But how will you get into the garage if your dad has no idea who you are?' Jamie asked.

'Easy! He keeps a spare set of keys under one of the garden gnomes,' Isaac said with a toothy grin.

'I'm pretty sure my parents have a broom in the garden shed too,' Jennifer said. Jemima's head shot up and she fixed Jennifer with a hard glare, but Jennifer simply swished her hair over her shoulder and looked the other way.

'We've got a nice mop that'd probably do the job,' Jamie added hopefully.

'I think if we have lots of options we're bound to find the perfect one. And lots of our parents will be at work right now, or getting things ready for tonight's festival, so . . . shall we split up and go and look?' Ivy asked.

'Let's not split up entirely. I'd say let's stick together in groups of two or three and meet back here in an hour,' Amethyst said. 'If you're able to get into your homes, I'd also suggest grabbing some salt from the kitchen. Then if you run into any trouble – like more crows – draw a circle of salt round yourself and *stay inside it* until you think it's safe again. OK? In the meantime, I'm going to think hard about what else you can all do when the festival begins – we can't just rely on me being able to get my real sister back.'

Everyone began to team up. Jamie, Jennifer and Jemima were an obvious team, although Jemima made it very clear that she was not their biggest fan. She refused to link arms like they always did and kept at least ten paces behind them as they walked towards Jamie's house first. Isaac and Eddie gave each other a simple nod to agree that they would be a team, and the other children paired up without any rowing or nonsense. They all knew there were bigger things afoot and that it would take every single one of them pulling together to make sure their plan came off without a hitch. After all, everyone was missing their parents terribly.

Maggie and Ivy would be a pair, seeing as they always did everything together. The only person left was Darla.

'Who are you teaming up with, Darla?' Maggie crouched down and asked the little girl.

'Mrs Unicorn,' she said over her thumb.

'Darla can stay here with me,' Amethyst said, hoisting Darla up into the air and then down on to her hip. 'We've got lots we can be getting on with here, haven't we? How do you feel about making some potions?'

Darla's thumb came out of her mouth to let her squeal, 'POTIONS?!'

'I'll take that as a big yes then!' Amethyst laughed, but then her face turned very serious as she looked at Maggie and Ivy and said, 'Once you've got your brooms, you come straight back. No dawdling, no extra-curricular activities, no side quests or adventures – no nonsense. OK? Straight. Back. Here.'

'Got it,' Ivy said. 'We promise.'

'It's not you I'm worried about . . .' Amethyst said, giving Maggie the side-eye.

'I'm insulted, Amethyst!' Maggie cried, feigning offence. 'Whatever makes you think I'm the one who would wander off unsupervised and cause nonsense?'

'Who was it who broke the dozen's circle again? And got captured by the witch?' Ivy asked, folding her arms across her chest.

'All right. Point taken. Although I think breaking the circle was a joint effort!'

'We'll be straight back, Amethyst,' said Ivy.

'Glad to hear it. Come on then, you. Let's make some memory potions. See if we can get my sister to remember the good old days,' Amethyst said to Darla.

Darla clapped her hands together and was so excited about making potions she almost let go of Mrs Unicorn.

Outside, the temperature had dropped and there was a bite in the air so fierce it practically had teeth. The children were still in their pyjamas, slippers and dressing gowns, and the sound of chattering teeth floated on the wind. Their breath was thick and foggy as they decided which homes to visit.

Ivy turned left to head towards her home. Her father kept the broom neatly in the garden shed along with his other gardening tools. Each one had its own hook on the wall; the bird feed was stored in boxes that were stacked in perfect rows, and even the lawnmower had its own little cubby hole to keep it protected. It was very clear where Ivy got her need for things to be kept tidy.

When they visited Maggie's garden shed on the other side of Hokum House, Ivy had expected the same chaos that filled Maggie's room, but instead it was relatively tidy, although that was probably only because there was nothing in it except a broom with far too few bristles, a pair of gardening gloves and a broken pair of shears.

'We're not much for gardening. Better for the wildlife this way, anyway!' Maggie shrugged, grabbing the broom despite its total uselessness.

'What happened to that thing?' Ivy asked, holding up her father's pristine gardening tool next to Maggie's for comparison.

'Dad got into a fight with a badger. It kept trying to get into our bins, so Dad went out there to shoo it away and the broom got the worst of it. We don't need it for sweeping up anyway! I'm sure it'll still fly fine.' Maggie put the broom between her legs and ran a few circles round Ivy, making loud race-car noises.

'I wouldn't want to chance falling out of the air,' Ivy said, pushing her glasses up her nose.

'Come on! Where's your sense of adventure?'

Ivy rolled her eyes at that question again. 'You know very well that I wasn't born with one,' she said drily, but Maggie ignored her.

'Speaking of which . . . why don't we go and see if anyone else needs our help?' Maggie wiggled her eyebrows.

'We promised Amethyst we'd be straight back! We literally just said it, not even five minutes ago.' Ivy began to walk back round to the front of Maggie's home and in the direction of Hokum House.

'I know, I know, but what if the witch tricks someone? And we're not there to help? We have magic now, Ivy! There might be something we could do!'

'Magic we have no idea how to use, Maggie. I wouldn't know the first thing about casting a spell to help someone.' Ivy held the broom under her arm and looked down at her fingers. If she concentrated hard she could almost feel the magic running through her veins. It felt like her blood was thick with something fizzy, and it made everything tingle when she thought about it hard enough. Her fingers began to turn a pale shade of pink and she quickly shook thoughts of magic away, in case she lost control and did something awful, like accidentally shrink Maggie's house to the size of a matchbox.

'I'm not saying anything is definitely going to happen, but . . . I dunno, I just think it'd be good to be on hand in case something did.' Maggie looked at Ivy with the puppy-dog eyes she usually deployed when trying to get her own way.

Ivy couldn't help but think that maybe Maggie was right. 'Well, a quick walk round the block and then back again. OK?' she conceded.

'That's all I ask, Ivy. That's all I ask.' Maggie grinned, slipping her arm through Ivy's and dragging her off down the street with a quick glance over her shoulder to make sure Amethyst wasn't watching.

The girls passed a few groups of children who had secured their parents' brooms and were making their way back towards Hokum House.

'See, Ivy? Nothing to worry about! Everyone's managing OK!' Maggie said, pointing with the handle end of her broom.

'Isaac and Eddie don't look like they're getting on too well.' Ivy gestured with her own broom towards the front lawn of Isaac's house. Eddie and Isaac were in a deep and heated discussion, waving their arms around wildly. Ivy and Maggie ventured over to investigate.

'When you said your dad keeps a spare key underneath a garden gnome, I assumed you meant there was only the one gnome! I wasn't expecting this!' Eddie crossed his arms, his face beading with sweat in frustration. As Ivy and Maggie approached, they could see what Eddie was talking about. Nearly every bit of the front lawn was covered in garden gnomes. Some of them were traditional garden gnomes holding fishing rods; others were holding cups of tea or riding bikes, and then there were some very odd ones, including one that looked like a zombie. All of them were freshly painted and impeccably clean, as if they were very well cared-for.

'Sorry. I forgot to mention that my dad is a bit of a garden-gnome enthusiast. Loves 'em.' Isaac shrugged unapologetically. 'Dunno why, though. I think they're a bit creepy. At least he doesn't keep them inside the house. He promised Mum they'd stay in the garden.'

'But this is just your front lawn . . .' Ivy said.

'I know. This only scratches the surface. He's got hundreds of them and they're all different too. There's even one that's sunbathing naked somewhere, but Mum often hides that one away out of sight.' Isaac sighed.

'What are the chances the key to the garage will be under one of the gnomes in the back garden?' Eddie asked, looking out at the sea of little red hats and white beards.

'It should definitely be one of these ones,' Isaac said. 'At least, I hope . . . Shall we get started then?'

Eddie squeezed his eyes tight shut and said, 'The sooner we start, the quicker we'll find it.' They hopped over the little red brick wall and began gently lifting the gnomes out of their spots, revealing brown and muddy patches from where they'd stood there for so long.

'Make sure to put them down exactly where you found them. My dad will kill me if he sees any of them have been moved or damaged.'

'Your dad won't ever know this was your doing. You could smash the whole lot up and he wouldn't know a thing,' Eddie said. Isaac thought about that for a moment, as he held one of the gnomes in his hand, thought about simply letting it go, thought about how good it might feel to throw it against the ground and watch it smash. But then he thought of his father's face and how it would crumple if he saw one broken into pieces. He didn't understand his dad's obsession with garden gnomes, but he did understand how much happiness they brought him. He felt the same way about collecting things in jars and studying creepy-crawlies and the slimy stuff on the surface of ponds. In that moment, he missed his father more than ever.

Isaac gently set the gnome down and continued to look for the key, when they suddenly heard it – a scream! It was so loud and so piercing that Maggie, Ivy, Eddie and Isaac had to cover their ears. Eddie almost dropped a gnome as his hands snapped up to his head, but he managed to catch it in the crook of his ankle without it breaking.

'What was that?' Ivy asked, whipping her head up and down the street to see if she could see who it could have been or what was happening. 'It came from near the house, didn't it?'

'Forget the broom. We'll have more than enough for Amethyst to choose from. Let's get back there now,' Maggie stated.

Together they ran as fast as they could until their lungs felt like they were burning from the cold autumn air. As they approached Hokum House, they could see Jennifer and Jamie bent over at the gate, catching their breath, both with tears streaming down their cheeks. It was only when Jamie gave a great heaving sob that they realized the tears weren't from the wind in their eyes – they were both crying.

'What's going on?' Amethyst asked as she ran with Darla in her arms from inside the house. She was followed by some of the other children.

'It's Jemima!' Jennifer cried, clutching a tiny salt shaker she'd taken from the spice rack in her home. 'The witch . . . ! She's got her!'

'Oh my goodness! She's taken her to the mountain?' Ivy shrieked.

'Did the crows get her like they got me?' Maggie asked, rolling up her sleeves, ready to fly to the rescue if she needed to.

'No!' Jamie said with a great gulp of air, trying to calm himself down. 'She didn't take her. She's just . . . got hold of her.'

'How?' asked Ivy.

'We were heading back here when she found this necklace. Like a choker made out of jagged green rocks,' Jamie said. 'I saw it at the same time Jemima did. It was in the grass at her feet, and as she reached down to get it I told her to be careful. Something about it was off – I could feel it in the air, and the crows started going wild. But Jemima ignored me and stuck her tongue out, and when she put it on . . .'

'It was instant. Like she was bewitched straight away! Her eyes were glowing green and so was the necklace,' Jennifer explained, holding her hands to her own throat, as if the witch might put one on her too.

'We screamed and ran away from her as fast as we could,' Jamie admitted sheepishly. 'We didn't know what else to do!'

'It sounds like Emerald has bewitched her.' Amethyst put Darla down but kept hold of her hand tightly.

'If she had been able to speak, maybe she'd have been able to scream for help,' Jamie snapped.

'I don't know what you're talking about,' said a voice from behind them. They turned to look up the street – and came face to face with Jemima. Her hair flowed out around her, moving through the air like she was underwater, but her eyes – no longer hazel – glowed a vicious shade of green. She was floating at least three metres off the ground, her arms gently bobbing like they were caught in a gentle tide, her feet slowly treading the air. 'I can use my voice,' Jemima said, but the voice most certainly didn't belong to Jemima.

It belonged to Emerald!

17

No Room on the Broom

The floating girl looked like Jemima, but at the same time completely different. It was her face, her body, her ginger hair and her baby-blue silk pyjamas, but there was an evil lurking behind it all, and that evil was most certainly coming from Emerald. Her voice spilled out of Jemima like poison.

'Let her go, Emerald!' Amethyst moved in front of the children with her arms outstretched, ready to protect them from any oncoming spells should she need to.

'Don't pretend you care about this one. You stole her voice!' Emerald snarled through Jemima's lips.

'How is she doing this?' Ivy asked.

'It's the necklace. A silly little power-throwing trick – the witch's equivalent of a ventriloquist throwing their voice. She's temporarily putting her powers into Jemima through that necklace.'

'Why didn't she eat Jemima's heart while she could?' Ivy asked.

'I don't think she actually came down here herself to plant that necklace,' Amethyst said, eyeing up a nearby crow that was eyeing her up right back.

'If you want a fight, come and face us like a *real* witch, you coward!' Maggie picked up a pebble and threw it towards Jemima. Her voice was scornful.

'Don't! You'll hurt Jemima!' Ivy stopped Maggie from throwing another pebble.

'You're on to something there, Maggie,' Eddie piped up. 'She's the *Crowood Witch*. We've been fearing her for centuries, and yet here she is, taking the form of a child?'

'Oh yeah . . . why isn't the almighty, all-powerful Emerald swooping in and taking one of us? Couldn't she simply destroy Crowood Peak in an instant with a click of her fingers if she wanted to?' Maggie sneered in Jemima's direction, but the girl's face remained blank. It was as if when Emerald wasn't speaking through her she went into a state of stillness, like a doll waiting to be played with.

Amethyst considered Maggie's challenge for a brief moment, and then a smile spread across her face when she knew what she could add. 'My sister is *scared*.' Amethyst raised her voice so that Emerald could hear her declaration.

'Scared? Don't be foolish, Amethyst,' Jemima snickered in Emerald's voice.

'But you are, aren't you? Otherwise you'd be here yourself, firing off your spells left, right and centre. Terrorizing the village. You'd be stealing not only the thirteenth child but also the fourteenth and fifteenth and so on and so forth until you'd had your fill.' Amethyst walked slowly but purposefully, step by step towards Jemima, while most of the watching children stayed back behind the gate of Hokum House. 'Something's stopping you, isn't it? What has got my sister so scared?'

'You've got it so very wrong, sister,' Emerald said, but her voice was quieter, less harsh – less *convincing*.

'Have I? Then why is it that with every step I take towards you, you seem to let Jemima float a little bit further away?' Amethyst asked, tutting. 'It's not like you to run from a fight.'

'Are you suggesting that I'm scared of *you*, Amethyst?' Emerald's voice was full of disdain, and she let out a cackle, but through Jemima's lips it didn't sound as terrifying as it had before. Or maybe she really *was* scared. 'You couldn't be further from the truth.'

'Then let the little girl go and face us like a proper witch.'

One of Jemima's eyebrows twisted upwards for a brief moment before her eyes flashed a vivid shade of green, and then went back to being their usual dull hazel. She began to fall through the air.

At exactly the same moment, Amethyst, Ivy and Maggie raised their hands and shot a stream of purple magic towards Jemima to break her fall. But as soon as their bolts of magic touched, the three of them were blasted backwards, falling to the ground themselves.

'Ouch!' Maggie said, rubbing the back of her head.

'Is Jemima OK?' Ivy sat up to see Jemima lying on her back on the ground, but she appeared physically unharmed – though she wondered what damage the Crowood Witch might have done to Jemima's mind.

Amethyst scrambled to her feet, ran to Jemima's side and quickly tore the necklace away from her throat, sending shards of green crystals skittering across the path. Maggie and Ivy quickly joined her to help hoist the unconscious Jemima off the ground by her arms and legs and carry her through the gates leading to Hokum House. Other children joined them and helped bring Jemima indoors.

'What happened then?' asked Jamie. He was holding a glass of water and a cold flannel, ready to give Jemima first aid. 'Why did you all fall over?'

'I'm not entirely sure,' Amethyst said. 'But . . . I think individually our magic isn't particularly strong, and since I hit Maggie and Ivy with that blast of magic my powers have been considerably weaker. My magic has somehow been split between the three of us, and when we tried to save Jemima together, the three shards reunited and it was much stronger than any of us were expecting.' She checked Jemima's pulse, as Jennifer and Jamie took her hands and gave each other a solemn look.

'She's going to be OK,' Amethyst added. 'She's just fainted. She must be completely exhausted. My sister isn't the easiest person to share a room with, let alone a brain – so she'll probably be out for a little while. But we'll make her comfortable – and I should probably return this.' She pulled the jar containing Jemima's voice from her coat pocket. 'I'm sorry now that I ever took it, but hopefully with a minor adjustment –' she held the golden jar up to the light – 'it'll make all the difference. She'll still be herself, mind. She has the power to turn these kind and golden words, all multiplied now, back into snarky red ones, but hopefully she'll make the right decision.' With that, Amethyst unscrewed the lid of the jar, which came off with a pop, and she tipped the contents into Jemima's open mouth. The children were quiet so they could hear the words whispering as they slipped past Jemima's lips. Jemima remained asleep, but her cheeks returned to their usual rosy colour and her face relaxed and softened.

'Now,' Amethyst said, 'let me see these brooms. And then we'll go through the rest of the plan.'

★

The selection of brooms laid across the living-room rug of Hokum House wasn't particularly varied. There was only one hardware shop in Crowood Peak, so most of the children's parents had purchased the same broom. And it was not ideal for flying – not a typical witch's broomstick at all. Amethyst surveyed the sorry bunch with a frown as she rubbed her chin.

'This one's broken.' Amethyst held up a poor excuse for a broom that had no bristles and almost half of the handle broken off.

'Yeah, I might have used it as a lightsabre when my brother challenged me to a fight,' said a boy called Archie, with a lopsided smile.

'This is no good for sweeping a garden, let alone trying to fly fifty metres in the air!' Amethyst tutted as she held up a broom that had a handle barely fifteen centimetres long. 'And this one is more of a twig than a broom!' she added, not even bothering to pick up one that really did look like it had fallen from a tree that morning rather than come from anyone's shed. 'I'm sorry, children, but I simply don't think there's one that will – wait a second.' Amethyst moved across the room to Jennifer. She was holding a broom by her side that looked more like a witch's broom than anything else in the room.

'Jennifer, that broom is *amazing*!'

'Thanks,' Jennifer said with a shy half-shrug. 'I made it for Halloween last year, but I didn't think it would be right, seeing as it's not an actual broom like the others.'

But Amethyst was delighted. 'This is *perfect*, Jennifer. This is exactly the sort of broom I would want for myself.'

Jennifer presented Amethyst with the broom as if she were handing over Excalibur, the legendary sword of King Arthur. The handle was made of a dark wood that Jennifer had sanded and polished until she could see herself in its surface. 'My mum's a carpenter, and she had an old staircase banister that she wasn't going to need so she let me have it,' she explained. 'And I collected the twigs at the end from some of the trees in Crowood Peak. It's nothing really. Just a silly little craft project.' Jennifer shook her head and stepped backwards, shying away from the children's gazes of admiration at her spectacular work.

'Jennifer, this is really quite something. You've made something truly incredible. And because it's made from Crowood trees it will be better at amplifying my magic,' Amethyst said happily.

'How?' asked Ivy.

'Remember that I told you that curses have a funny way of attaching themselves to things? It's not only curses. All magic finds a way of sticking to things it shouldn't, but trees especially. Trees are old and have often been around for so long they've seen more magic than anything else. This bundle of twigs probably contains more magic than the three of us put together! Old magic too. This broom is the real deal.' Amethyst turned to Jennifer, who was beaming, and asked, 'Would you mind awfully if I borrowed it?'

'You mean . . . a real witch is actually going to fly on my broomstick?' Jennifer looked at Amethyst with big, round, glistening eyes.

'Hopefully two witches, if I manage to pull off this plan without a hitch.'

'Wow . . .' Jennifer said breathlessly. 'That is too cool.'

'Is that a yes?'

'A big one!' Jennifer giggled, and everyone joined in.

'So, what exactly is the plan then, Amethyst?' asked Eddie, who always had his thinking cap firmly on his head. 'Because if you're right and your magic has, in fact, been split between you, Maggie and Ivy . . . surely you won't be able to defeat Emerald on your own. You'll need all your magic for that, which means –'

'We'll have to come with you!' Maggie interrupted, stepping forward with her chest puffed out. 'We can help, can't we, Ivy?'

Ivy joined her friend. 'That makes me awfully nervous, but . . . I'm prepared to do whatever it takes to stop Emerald. And if that means using this magic you've given me, then I'm willing to do so.'

Amethyst shook her head.

'Just one problem . . .' Jennifer said, taking the broom from Amethyst and holding it up lengthways. 'There's no room on the broom! This will only hold Amethyst, and Emerald at a push. It's not designed to hold four people at once!'

'You know what you need to do then, Amethyst.' Ivy's voice was low and calm.

Amethyst was quiet for a moment, her forehead crinkled in confusion, but then the crinkles ironed out with sudden horror. 'Absolutely no way. That is far too dangerous and is not happening.' She snatched the broom away and walked towards the front door. 'I'd rather take my chances with Emerald alone than put anyone in more danger than necessary.'

'What are you both talking about?' Maggie asked.

'Eddie's idea is to lure Emerald here. So she has no choice but to face the three of us: face all of Amethyst's magic, not just a third of it,' Ivy explained.

'Clearly that's why she was so scared to come here alone before,' Eddie continued. 'She knows the prophecy. She knows you have the power to defeat her again, like you did before.'

'That's true, Amethyst,' said Ivy. 'The first chance she got, she took off and flew to the mountain. If she genuinely thought she could crush you with one spell, she would have done it in that instant. Instead, she ran.'

195

'That's true, but . . . the last time I defeated her, it . . . it . . .'
Amethyst began to stutter, clutching the handle of the broom
to her chest like it was a beloved childhood toy.

'It was what?' Ivy pushed.

'It was an accident,' Amethyst mumbled.

There was a stunned silence. All the children looked at
Amethyst as though she'd just admitted she was, in fact, the
evil sister and it was she who was responsible for eating the
hearts of twelve children.

'What do you mean it was an accident?!' Eddie asked,
almost through gritted teeth.

'Please don't be angry with me.' Amethyst's eyes began to
brim with tears.

'Just tell us what happened last time around, Amethyst.
There must have been something you did that defeated her.
Something you can do again!' Ivy said hopefully.

'Not really.' Amethyst sobbed, dashing the last scrap of
hope Ivy had. 'All I did was hug her.'

'You . . . *hugged* her?' Maggie asked, and Amethyst nodded,
unable to meet any of the children's eyes.

'Emerald kept throwing spells at me, which I blocked as
best I could until she had me on my knees and I couldn't fight
any more. Then she got very close, close enough to finish me
off, and . . . I reached out and hugged my sister, knowing it
would probably be the last thing I ever did. I still loved her
despite everything she had done and how evil she had

become. She was still my twin sister and I knew this wasn't really her. It was the curse. All of a sudden it was like she was melting in my arms. She withered away and shrank until there was just an old black dress on the floor of this house, with something wriggling about inside it. When I untangled the mess of fabric, inside was my sister, but she was –'

'A cat,' Maggie finished.

'I don't know how I did that spell. I remember hugging her and wishing that she was harmless. I wished so hard that she would no longer be hell-bent on eating the hearts of children. I wished that she was unable to inflict any more pain, and all of a sudden she was no longer able to cause any more suffering because she was a little kitty. That bit was accidental magic and I have no idea how to replicate that spell. All I know is that a little bit of sisterly love went a very long way.' Amethyst finished her story with a long, hard sniff. 'Then before the night was over, I used the magic of the moon to tie her to the house.'

'Which is why you think if you can get her to remember the bond you had when you were kids, and how you used to go flying together, it might do the same thing as it did before?' Eddie asked, and Amethyst nodded slowly. There was a collective grumble and groan.

'Hey now!' Maggie raised her voice. 'I trust Amethyst. Besides . . . what other option do we have? The Crowood Witch is ready to snatch one of us and turn all the grown-ups in the village into heart-eating monsters. If we didn't have Amethyst, we'd definitely be doomed to that fate. And remember, there are going to be other things we can do too – we can help to weaken Emerald, stand together to save our village.'

'Maggie is right.' Ivy nodded. 'Amethyst's plan isn't just a good plan – it's also our *only* plan. And I'm ready to give it the best shot we can. Unless anyone else has any better ideas?' This time the children were silent – even Eddie wasn't able to think of a better plan. 'Exactly. So let's listen to Amethyst now, find out what else she wants us to do, and then we're going to carry out her plan as best we can. And if it doesn't work . . .'

'At least we'll die trying,' Maggie said.

A hush filled the living room of Hokum House. The room was devoid of sound but filled with something else. A lot of fear, but also a little bit of hope.

'This *can* work. We just need to pull together and believe in each other. But, most of all, we need to believe in Amethyst.' Ivy's smile was a little nervous, but it seemed to do the trick. Amethyst smiled back, looking a lot braver.

'Thank you, Ivy.' Amethyst wiped away her tears. 'Now, it's time to defeat my sister.'

18
Good Luck, Amethyst

The older children made everyone pair up and form two straight lines outside the house. Ivy stood at the front with her pink walkie-talkie and Maggie stood at the rear with her green one – they had decided not to use their mind-reading in case it weakened their magic or drew Emerald to them.

'Ready to move? Over,' Ivy asked.

'Ready as we'll ever be. Over,' Maggie replied from the back of the group.

'Time to move out!' Ivy called.

Together, the children marched through the gate of Hokum House and to each child's home to change their clothes as fast as they possibly could and collect any salt they hadn't already found. If there were grown-ups around – not everyone was out or at work – then another child found some clothes from their home to help. Working together. No splitting up this time. It was too easy for the witch to get them that way.

It was a tradition that everyone in the village wore green to the festival, which would make it much easier for them to blend in and less likely to be spotted by the witch. So every child dressed from head to toe in green; most of them had on traditional green cloaks and coats that covered whatever they wore underneath, but some wore green dresses or green T-shirts and trousers. It wasn't just any kind of green either. Everything they wore was *emerald* green. In the same way that most families have a box of Halloween costumes or Christmas jumpers, every family in Crowood Peak had a box of green clothes stashed away in the back of a cupboard or in the loft or garage. Now that the festival was upon them, they weren't hard for the children to find.

'Right, has everyone changed? Good. OK.' Amethyst was still wearing her purple coat, but her face looked sickly green. 'Oh, goodness, I've suddenly got very nervous.'

'Do we really have to do this?' Jennifer sounded worried.

'Hopefully it won't come to this. But my plan is risky. I'm going to go up to the mountain and try my hardest to talk some sense into Emerald. If that works and I get her on to the broom, I'll bring her down here when she's ready, to where Maggie and Ivy and I can combine our magic to try to get the evil out of her heart. But if something goes wrong and she makes a run for it, we need you all to be in the middle of the village. It's the only guarantee that she'll come where we need her,' Amethyst said apologetically. She swallowed, not wanting to say the next bit, but knowing everyone was thinking it. 'She needs a child's heart, tonight. But if you all stay together, she won't get one!' she added determinedly.

'Do you honestly think she'll come to the festival?' Jamie asked.

'Are you kidding? Every child from Crowood Peak standing in the middle of the main square, wearing the Crowood Witch's colour, without a single protection spell to ward her off?' Isaac rolled his eyes. 'Oh yeah. She'll turn up.'

'It's like we're just offering up all our hearts on a platter,' Eddie remarked.

'Don't worry. If it comes to that, as soon as she gets close enough I'll swoop in and get her on this broom. I won't be able to take her too far away, though – I'll have to fly close to the village square to make sure I can get to Ivy and Maggie. Hopefully I'll get through to her up on the mountain, and she'll let us remove the evil from her. Then none of you will ever be put in any danger. I know it's not the most solid plan A, but I'd rather try that first.' Amethyst sighed and turned to Maggie and Ivy. 'Now, tell me again what you need to do.

Just so I'm one hundred per cent certain you know what's expected of you.'

'As soon as you land in the middle of the village square with Emerald – who we hope has already remembered what it's like to be good and happy and carefree, and not a heart-eating, devil-worshipping, wicked witch – we'll be there ready to join forces with you as you envelop Emerald in a *hope* spell,' Maggie said.

'A spell that's designed to restore someone's hope when they've lost it. To cast said spell, what we need to do is think of the happiest thing we can possibly think of – the thing that fills us with the most hope for the future. So I'm going to think of becoming a scientist who finds cures for things that make people sick.' Ivy's eyes sparkled at this thought.

'And I'm going to think of the day my books are on the shelves of the Crowood Peak bookshop alongside my dad's, when he finally gets one of his novels published too. Maybe we'll even write a book together one day.' Maggie couldn't help but grin at the idea of her and her father telling stories together for the whole world to read.

'Good. Good. OK.' Amethyst nodded. 'Right, well . . . best be off,' she said quietly, as she mounted the broom.

All the children crowded around and patted her on the shoulder or squeezed her hands, and Darla wrapped her arms round one of her legs and hugged tightly. 'Come on, little one.

I'll be back before you know it. Remember the potion we made? I've sprayed it on my wrists to help convince Emerald to be good! Look after Mrs Unicorn for us both.' Amethyst bent down and kissed the top of Darla's head while Maggie and Ivy gently coaxed her away. 'Here I go. I'll see you later in the square. Good luck, everyone.'

'Amethyst,' Ivy said, just before she kicked off the ground and into the air, 'no matter what happens, you'll always be the best witch we've ever known.'

'Yeah. We'll never forget what you're doing for us, Amethyst,' said Maggie.

'Hey, this battle isn't over yet. Don't give up too soon.' And with that, Amethyst pushed off from the ground with a fierce kick of her leg and whooshed up into the air on Jennifer's handmade broom.

'Come on, gang,' said Maggie, her face turning fierce as she rolled up her emerald sleeves. 'Let's go and catch ourselves a witch.'

19

The Moon Appears

Amethyst flew as fast as she could through the dark autumn sky. The higher she got, the more her heart began to race, as she scanned the sky for the full moon. She knew her sister was waiting for the moment when she could make the biggest spectacle, inflict the most damage, terrorize everyone completely. And Emerald would surely know from her messenger crows that everyone would be gathered in the square for the festival, so Amethyst knew that's when she would strike.

The blue moon hadn't appeared yet, which meant she still had time . . . but not much. The air suddenly became thick with black smoke and an earthy smell that Amethyst knew was the scent of her sister's magic. Her own magic smelled of sugar and fruit – *silly magic*, she thought. Her sister had always been able to cast spells with strength and might, while she was stuck bewitching household items to bake cakes and biscuits, or making potions to help injured squirrels and other wildlife. Emerald had always teased Amethyst when they were children – though it hadn't stopped her eating all the goodies! Now Amethyst's magic needed to do something truly powerful. Hopefully, a third of it would be enough, but if not, then she trusted Maggie and Ivy to come through when she needed them most.

Amethyst landed delicately on the flat surface of the mountain. She looked at the jagged stones and boulders that were left behind where the peak of the mountain used to be – before the Crowood Witch had split it with her magic and sent it hurtling towards the village below. It was desolate and bleak, and left Amethyst feeling cold all the way through to her bones – the kind of cold that doesn't leave for a long time, even after you should have warmed up. That was the effect her sister had now that her soul was almost entirely wicked, and Amethyst was yet to come face to face with her.

But when Emerald did appear, Amethyst was shocked by what she saw.

'Well, well, well. Come to learn some proper magic from a proper witch, sister?' Emerald asked. Her words were cruel, but she didn't look nearly as fierce as she had when she'd burst through the roof of Hokum House. She looked completely drained of energy and magic.

Amethyst glanced towards the great swirling smoke hurricane above them and wondered exactly what it was costing Emerald to keep the forgetting spell going for this long. Almost two days had passed since she had cast it. Amethyst's own spell had made her feel weak, and she had only made the village forget a legend most people thought was a fairy tale anyway. Emerald's spell had made all the adults in the village forget their own children! Years of special memories that were vivid and bright in everyone's minds – full of hope and love and joy. Trying to erase memories like that took seriously strong magic, and it was clearly taking its toll on Emerald.

'Emerald, it's time to stop. I don't believe you're completely wicked, nor that you cannot resist the curse. You've simply forgotten what it's like to be happy. But you're not alone now. I'm here.' Amethyst took a tentative step towards her sister, broom still in hand.

Emerald threw her head back and cackled up to the sky, and the cloud above them gave a low rumble in response. 'I know happiness,' Emerald barked. 'It's *this*! Happiness is *power*. Something you'd know nothing about. You have barely enough power to rid a hedgehog of fleas. I can control an entire village!'

'Not an *entire* village,' Amethyst said. 'There are children down there who aren't affected by your magic, Emerald. And they won't let you take over the minds of their parents without a fight.'

'Children?' Emerald cackled once again, this time with her teeth bared. 'What on earth are a bunch of snivelling, snotty children going to do that could possibly stop *me*, the greatest and most powerful witch ever?' As she picked her teeth with her long, claw-like nails, she pulled a small bone out, most likely from a rat or a mouse. Amethyst realized her sister wasn't going to shake off three hundred years spent as a cat right away . . .

'Don't you remember what we were like as children, Emerald?' Amethyst asked, trying to keep the desperation out of her voice – she knew her sister would see that as a weakness.

'I don't think I ever was a child. Not really.' Emerald looked away from her sister, turning her attention back to the spell, but Amethyst was grateful that she was proving a distraction. Every second that Emerald wasn't pouring magic into the spell was a moment that gave Amethyst hope.

'Don't be so silly, Emerald. Or in fact . . . *do* be silly. You were silly once. You used to play games and make faces and dream up stories . . . and it made us happy. Once upon a time, it made *you* happy. Once upon a time, you liked being my sister. Before the curse.'

'You were always a thorn in my side,' Emerald said quietly, barely audible above the roaring wind, and Amethyst took that as a sign that she didn't really mean it.

'Oh, don't you remember how much fun we used to have?'

'No,' Emerald lied.

'You do. I can see it in your eyes. Just take one flight with me. Like old times. I'll even let you drive.' Amethyst held out the broom to Emerald.

'What is that wretched little thing?' Emerald sneered, but Amethyst could tell her voice was growing softer.

'Something one of the children made.' Amethyst looked fondly at the broom, seeing all the love and care Jennifer had put into it.

'It's ghastly.' Emerald tried to sneer, but her eyes were on the broom, following it wherever Amethyst moved it, transfixed.

'But it *fliieeess*,' Amethyst teased.

For a moment, Emerald's eyes became round and soft, just like when they were children. But that was quickly replaced by a look of fierce rage. 'This is a trick, isn't it?' she hissed, and pointed a bony finger towards the village. 'This is something you've cooked up with those disgusting, putrid little pipsqueaks down there.'

'No, Emerald.' Amethyst tried to remain calm, but her nerves were on fire, her whole body was tingling with the terror of what her sister might do next.

'It is! I can tell! You're trying to get me to look back on the *good old days* and remember when things used to be rosy, so they can be rosy once again! All because I'm more powerful now than you'll ever be! That's it, isn't it? You're jealous that *you* weren't the chosen one.' Emerald spun round with a swish of her dress and began to walk away.

'What do you mean?' Amethyst shivered as the temperature plummeted. The cold of the rock beneath her feet seemed to penetrate her shoes and freeze her toes.

'You're furious that the curse wasn't passed to you!' Emerald spat. 'But let me tell you, sister. You'd never be able to handle this. Every waking moment of my life is filled with *fury*!' She screamed up to the stars, tears beginning to fall fast from her black eyes. 'I've never felt power like it.'

'You're angry all the time? Emerald, it sounds exhausting. And sad. Don't you ever just want . . . to feel safe? And loved?'

'And weak?'

'Love isn't weakness, Emerald. Don't you remember how strong we used to feel when we were together? As a team?'

'If that's true, then why didn't you come after me?' Emerald asked, suddenly calmer and quieter. The question was like a punch to Amethyst's gut.

'What? Emerald . . .' Amethyst was scared the thudding of her heart would cause an avalanche, it was beating so loudly. 'The day after our birthday I woke up and you were simply gone. Vanished. Our parents told me they had sent you away to protect us all, and you had run. They said you didn't want to be found, and none of us knew where you had gone – it was months before I felt drawn here. If I'd known then that you'd come straight here, I would have raced to be with you, helped rid you of that curse before it took hold of you. I would have followed you to the ends of the earth.'

'LIES!' Emerald threw her arms up to the sky and green lightning shot from her hands. The blast was so violent that Amethyst was knocked over and on to her back. As she dropped the broomstick it rolled towards Emerald and stopped at her feet. Her black eyes looked down and a devious smile crawled across her lips.

'EMERALD, NO!' Amethyst yelled, but it was too late. Emerald snatched up the broom and flew past Amethyst. She was so quick that Amethyst could do nothing but watch as Emerald became a speck in the distance, heading for the village below.

Amethyst ran to the edge, watching the trail of black smoke zoom down towards the village square, which was brightly lit with hundreds of warm fairy lights. Amethyst could just hear the music from a band and the hum and laughter of the unsuspecting people who were about to feel the wrath of her sister. She thought of the children, standing together, waiting for her to come and save them, and how scared they would be when Emerald arrived there without her. What would

Emerald do if she didn't get there in time to stop her? Amethyst felt sick. Her magic was already weak. A flight down to the village would weaken her further . . . How would she protect the children of Crowood Peak?

She suddenly felt a light upon her face, which soothed her so much that she closed her eyes and enjoyed the warmth for a moment. Then a feeling of calm came over her.

When she opened her eyes again, she cast her gaze up to the sky where the moon was big and round . . . the thirteenth full moon. The blue moon.

20
Stone

The celebrations for the festival were in full swing. The children could hear the music of the folk band playing and could smell the sweet and sickly scent of sticky toffee long before they reached the main square. The trees were bare and fairy lights had replaced the fallen orange and brown leaves, which had been used to make the garlands wrapped round every lamp post. They wanted to get closer but they hung back in the shadows, feeling nervous about what lay ahead. Well, nearly all of them felt nervous . . .

'Is there time to stop for biscuits?' Maggie asked, spotting the stand she usually spent most of the festival near because

Mrs Anderson liked her and let her sample every flavour. Her tummy was beginning to rumble, and a chocolate-orange cookie would certainly hit the spot.

'Once this is over, I will make you all the biscuits you want, but we have more important things to deal with right now,' Ivy said, tutting.

'But if we don't make it through this, you will have deprived me of eating one final biscuit,' Maggie protested.

'If we don't make it through this, biscuits will be the least of your worries,' Ivy said.

'Good point. OK, is everyone ready? Does everyone remember the plan of action?' Maggie looked over her shoulder at the horde of children, their faces slowly becoming the same colour as their outfits, the nervous energy palpable. All their forgetful parents were crowded in the centre of the village, playing games, dancing, eating, drinking and being incredibly merry, while their children were alone, desperately wanting to go home and be held and told bedtime stories and feel safe once more. One by one they each took a deep breath and nodded at Maggie, who then waved them forward. Ivy followed at the rear, her walkie-talkie in her hand in case it was needed.

The children stepped out from the shadows and began to walk towards the grassy area in the centre of the square where the folk band was playing on a small bandstand. At first, no one paid them much attention, but within seconds there began to be murmurings from the crowd. Grown-ups moved out of their way, creating a path for the long line of lonely children dressed in green.

'Who are they?' Mrs Moody whispered.

'Where have they come from?' Mr Woodman asked.

'Why are they here? No one in Crowood has any children! Nasty creatures . . .' Each whisper felt a dagger to the children's hearts. All of these people that they knew and loved. People who had helped them with their homework, taught them at school, played with them and offered their advice . . . all of them had forgotten them. Some of the children felt tears pricking the backs of their eyes, and others kept their eyes down altogether. They knew they had a job to do. A very important one that might be the difference between life and death. Between their parents forgetting forever and remembering again.

The band stopped playing with a violent shriek of a violin and the band members stepped down and went off for a break. Maggie and Ivy climbed up on to the bandstand and the other children made a circle round the outside, all facing outwards. Then, exactly as they had planned, they threw salt on the grass, making a full circle of it round the bandstand, and all held hands. A crowd began to gather, and the children were soon facing their parents.

'Elijah Brown. Orla Cartwright. Clarence Cauldwell . . .' Maggie and Ivy began to chant the names of the twelve children that the Crowood Witch had snatched three hundred years before. 'Ophelia Drake. Laurence Drake. David Durkin . . .' One by one, the children began to chant the names together, getting louder and louder until they were all yelling them at the top of their lungs. 'Claudia Fleming. Gwen Harking. Peter Pound.' The grown-ups looking on began to step backwards, away from the children, passing looks of confusion between them. Some were amused, thinking it must be part of the festivities, completely unaware of the tragedies that had taken place three centuries ago. Tragedies that were about to take place once more. 'Prudence Pound! Orin Thomas! Wilbur Tweedle!'

Together, the children chanted the names over and over and over, raising their joined hands up into the air and holding on to each other's palms and fingers so tightly their knuckles turned white. Amethyst had taught them that the past had a nasty way of repeating itself, and that there was a kind of magic in remembrance, which helped people learn from past mistakes. All of the nerves and fear and anger and sadness they had been feeling rose up within them and into their voices.

None of them saw the witch coming. But suddenly she was there, when just a moment before she hadn't been, and the only thing that alerted them to her presence was the great *THWACK* that rang out across the square as she landed on the metal roof of the bandstand. The claws of her feet cut through the tin like it was butter. She had come from above, with no need to cross their salt circle. Her evil was in there with them!

The crowd of grown-ups jumped – some screamed and ran away from the bandstand, but some stayed, transfixed by the scene before them. Emerald rooted herself firmly on the top of the bandstand with her claws and slowly uncurled into a standing position, with Jennifer's broom grasped in her hands like she was wielding an axe. The children remained inside the bandstand, quiet and trembling, still gripping each other's hands, their nails digging into each other's palms. No one wanted to let go.

'Adults of Crowood Peak!' The smoke descended on the grown-ups and suddenly their eyes became glazed. 'These children are not to be trusted. They are here to cause mayhem and disrupt your happy, quiet and peaceful lives. They want to latch on to you and suck out your energy, money and time until you're nothing but shells – ghosts of the people you once were,' the witch cried.

'It's not true!' Maggie yelled, a tear slipping down her face as she looked towards Max, who was hanging on to the witch's every word.

'She's lying! Please listen to us!' Ivy screamed at Bill, who couldn't tear his eyes away from the witch above him.

'SILENCE!' Emerald raised the broom high above her head.

'Where's Amethyst?' Eddie whispered on Ivy's left.

'She promised she'd be here,' Darla said, clutching Mrs Unicorn and snivelling.

'She'll be here,' Ivy said firmly, looking up to the sky for any sign of a flash of purple.

'Why isn't Emerald casting her worst spell?' Maggie whispered to Ivy. 'If she wanted these adults to turn into monsters and eat our hearts, then why isn't she doing it yet?'

Ivy leaned forward and craned her neck to try to see the witch on the roof of the bandstand. Then a thought occurred to her. 'She's weak. Maggie, Emerald is weak!'

'Yeah ...' Maggie nodded, the penny dropping. 'If Amethyst gets weak from using too much magic, Emerald must do too.'

'I bet that spell she's casting to make our dads and all the other parents forget us is draining all of her energy!' Ivy let go of Maggie's hand and rolled up her sleeves. 'She wants to cast that spell but she can't. Now's our chance to cast the hope spell, Maggie. We have to take it.'

'But Amethyst isn't here!' Maggie said, rubbing her hands together; they had gone numb in the bitter evening chill.

'I know, but we have to do something or we'll run out of time. We don't know how quickly Emerald will regain her strength, but we do have *two thirds* of Amethyst's magic. It has to be cast before the moon is full!'

'OK. Remember what Amethyst said, then. Think of the happiest and most hopeful thought you can,' Ivy said.

'Three . . .' Maggie said. She concentrated hard on the books she'd one day write, and her hands began to glow purple.

'. . . two . . .' Ivy said, thinking of the people she'd one day help with her incredible groundbreaking work in science, and her hands began to glow and spark too.

'. . . one – GET HER!' they yelled.

Together, they hopped over the metal railing of the bandstand and landed with a dull thud on the dewy grass. They ran a few paces and then turned quickly towards the witch, who still had the broom raised above her head. With her hands full she was unable to blast them with a spell, so Maggie and Ivy took their chance and summoned up every single fragment of magic they could feel running in their veins and shot it towards Emerald. Streams of purple flowed out of their fingers towards her. She gave a shriek of horror and dropped the broom, which tumbled off the bandstand roof and on to the ground. The purple streams wound themselves round her like ropes and tied her arms to her sides. Once Maggie and Ivy saw she'd been successfully bound with their hopeful thoughts, they let their arms fall to their sides, feeling exhausted but triumphant.

'We did it!' Maggie jumped up and down and raised her fists in the air and ran in circles like she'd just scored a winning goal. There was some scattered applause from the other children – but not everyone was convinced the battle was won, including Ivy.

'I don't think it's over. This doesn't seem . . . right . . .'

'Fools! Amethyst has sent children to do what only a witch stronger than me can do!' Emerald jeered, and as she did so, the ropes made of purple magic turned green. Instead of breaking out of the bonds, Emerald simply slipped out of them, like a snake shedding its skin, and then picked them up in her hands as if they were whips. She looked wild and excited, and the children's confusion turned to fear. Most began to scream and huddle together.

'Oh no! We've made her stronger! She's taken some of our magic and turned it into her own!' Ivy whimpered, running back into the middle of the bandstand for cover, narrowly avoiding the snap of the green magic whip as Emerald began to lash the magic wildly to and fro. Her lip curled as she whisked the ends of the ropes across the salt circle, scattering it everywhere.

'I am indestructible!' Emerald cried as she snapped the whip again and caught the ankle of a woman trying to run. Maggie and Ivy watched as the woman's ankle turned a dusty-grey colour where the green whip wrapped tightly round it. The grey spread all the way up her body, right to the tips of her outstretched fingers as she reached for help. It ran up her face and to the very ends of her hair until, finally, the woman was made entirely of stone. Her terrified expression was solidified in rock for evermore.

'Mumma . . .' Darla whimpered, and stretched out her arms towards the woman. Eddie quickly turned Darla towards him and tried to distract her with Mrs Unicorn, but it was too late – Darla began to wail for her lost mother. Emerald's laugh rose into the darkening sky and she began to snap both whips furiously in every direction she possibly could, continuing to cackle with delight. The screams grew quieter as more and more people were turned to statues.

'Dad! Bill! RUN!' Maggie had spotted Bill and Max crouching down behind a stall that had been selling cards and paper crafts.

'Dad?' Ivy's head snapped round to follow Maggie's desperate gaze, and she threw caution to the wind and ran to them. 'Dad! Max! Go! Run back to the house! Or leave town! Just go!'

Bill and Max looked at them with furrowed brows, perplexed as to how two strange little girls knew their names and why they were so desperate to help them more than anyone else. But the sound of the Crowood Witch squealing with delight as she took the breath from people's bodies and turned them into statues was enough to make them stop and listen. That was until Emerald spotted Maggie and Ivy.

'Ahhh! You two again! What is it I heard you call yourselves when I used to hide under your bed? Ah, yes. *The Double Trouble Society*. Up to your old tricks, eh?'

'Leave them alone.' Max raised his trembling voice and stood in front of Maggie.

'They're only children,' Bill said, swooping Ivy out of the way behind him. Maggie and Ivy shared a small smile. Even when their dads didn't recognize them, they would still protect them. It gave them both the little shred of hope they needed.

'Oh, what a touching moment,' Emerald mocked. 'What a shame that moments are only fleeting.' She pulled back her arms as far as they would go and hurled the whips forward. Maggie and Ivy flinched as Emerald's perfect aim snapped one whip round Max's waist and the other round Bill's neck.

'NO!' Maggie and Ivy screamed blood-curdling screams, but it was too late. Their fathers turned their heads to cast one last look at each other before those looks were etched in stone. As Emerald snatched her whips back and began to swing them at other unsuspecting adults, Maggie and Ivy came out from behind their fathers.

'Dad! Dad, can you hear me? It's me! It's me, it's your Maggie!' Maggie wrapped her arms round Max where Emerald's whip had caught him.

'It's no use, Maggie. He's gone. They're . . . they're both gone.' Ivy reached out and wrapped her hand round her father's rough, cold fingers. No warmth was left in him. He was no longer human. No longer alive. Just a statue in the main square on which birds would perch and future children would graffiti, not knowing that he was once a man. A brilliant mind. A loving father. Ivy stepped backwards and felt something hard under her foot. She looked down to see her father's glasses. He couldn't see without his glasses. She picked them up and turned them over in her hands, not knowing what else to do.

As she looked down, she realized that her hands were glowing purple. She dropped the glasses on the ground. Everything she was feeling, all the anger and sadness and love, was making her magic stronger.

'*ARGH!*' Ivy sent a wild ball of crackling, flaming purple magic at Emerald. The witch had her back turned and it hit her square between the shoulders. She cried out in pain and dropped both whips, which fizzled into nothingness as they fell to the ground, leaving patches of charred grass beneath them. For a moment, the main square went quiet. The children round the bandstand had broken their circle and were now huddled as closely together as they could. Most of the adults had run as far away as possible, and those who were left in the square were now made of stone. The only sound left was Ivy's voice.

'HOW COULD YOU?!' she roared as she sent yet another purple orb at Emerald.

This time Emerald heard it coming and swiped it away with a blocking spell just before it struck her shoulder. 'Oh, the little one has found some courage, has she? Now, which one are you? Double? Or Trouble?' she said evilly.

'What happened to you?' Ivy sobbed. 'What happened to you to make you this way? This *evil*?'

Emerald flashed a toothy grin. 'I've always been evil.'

'No. You weren't born evil. You were cursed, but you could break it. You don't *have* to be this way.'

'Why wouldn't I want to remain this powerful forever? Why would I want to be weak like you?!' the witch howled. She flicked her wrist, creating a small ball of fire in her hand, which she turned round and round with her fingers.

'You've still got Amethyst! She loves you and there's a part of you that still loves her too.'

'Love?! LOVE?!' Emerald sneered and wound her arms round each other, and the ball of flames grew to the size of a beach ball.

With one final shriek, she lifted the flames above her head and thrust the ball with all her might towards Ivy and Maggie. The green flames shone in both their eyes as they clung to each other. Surely, they thought, this was their final moment . . .

Or was it? Even with their eyes squeezed shut, they could still see the glow of the flames behind their eyelids. But nothing happened!

They tentatively opened their eyes . . . and there was Amethyst!

She looked unlike they'd ever seen her before. Her long white hair and pale skin glowed bright and ethereal in the moonlight. In fact, she looked like she *was* the moonlight. She floated above Emerald with a tranquil look on her face.

'Amethyst . . .' For the first time, Emerald was shocked. Her jaw flapped open and closed as she took in her sister's radiance and power. 'How . . . did you . . . You can't stop me. You know you can't.' Emerald held up her hands, ready to fight Amethyst, but Maggie and Ivy could see that she was shaking.

'Sister.' Amethyst smiled gently. 'You forget what kind of witch I am.'

Ivy and Maggie both gasped and grinned.

'Amethyst is a *moon witch*!' Maggie jumped into the air and floated up to Amethyst, circled her twice, cheering and whooping, and then came back down to Ivy's side.

'That's how you defeated her before! The moon was at its fullest when you hugged her and wished as hard as you could!' Ivy shouted. 'You didn't realize it then, because you weren't as skilled with your magic! But now –'

'Now I have three hundred years of practice under my belt.' Amethyst grinned, and she glowed a little bit brighter.

'You're still just a moon witch!' Emerald cried. 'Still no match for the likes of me!' She sent a ball of green lightning towards Amethyst, but her sister simply waved a single finger and it turned to purple bubbles, which floated through the air and burst with satisfying little pops.

'Maybe not when you're at your strongest, dear sister. But you've used almost every bit of energy you have to make this village forget. And now you've trapped them in stone. You've barely got any magic left to hurt me.'

Amethyst floated down to the roof of the bandstand, still keeping a little bit of distance from her sister. 'I don't want to hurt you. I don't want to turn you into a cat for another three hundred years. I just want my sister back.' She raised her hand and the broomstick jumped up from the grass below and into her open palm. Then Amethyst shot a purple spark towards her sister. It hit her firmly in the centre of her chest and knocked her backwards off the bandstand roof, but before she could hit the floor, Amethyst zoomed round to catch Emerald on the back of the broom, and together they sped off towards the moon.

21

Two Sisters on a Broom

Emerald tried to fly away, but her fingers began to fizz and sparkle on and off like a sputtering engine unable to start.

'No! NO!' she cried, quickly realizing she had very little magic left.

'Emerald,' Amethyst said calmly, looking over her shoulder at her sister, 'if you tried to fly now, you would fall from the sky and splat on to the ground below in seconds.'

Emerald leaned backwards away from Amethyst and held on to the broom behind her, not wanting any kind of close contact with the witch who was trying to rid her of the darkness that had corrupted her for so long. She was desperately trying to steady herself, but she kept wobbling.

'If you shake this broom one more time, I'm going to kick you off it and into the darkness below. Now, for goodness' sake, hold on to me and relax!' Amethyst laughed, knowing Emerald had no other choice. Emerald grunted and snaked her arms round her sister's waist. Amethyst bent forward and thought, *Fast.* The broom went from really quite fast to a frightening, dangerous, almost-can't-quite-hold-on kind of lightning-speed. Amethyst could feel Emerald's arms squeeze tighter and then, to her great surprise, she heard a sound escaping from Emerald's mouth.

'Did you just laugh?!' Amethyst called over her shoulder above the wind as it whooshed through their long hair. 'Not a cackle, but an actual proper giggle?!'

'No!' Emerald shot back. Amethyst pulled the broom handle upwards and curved them into a perfect loop-the-loop through the sky, leaving a trail of glittering purple magic in their wake. Emerald heard a scream of pure delight and it took her a while to realize it was coming from her own mouth. Then the scream turned into a belly laugh that she could no longer keep contained. 'OK, maybe,' she conceded between chuckles. 'But only for a second. Nothing has changed, sister. When we get back down on to the ground there will be hell to pay.'

'Oh, I have no doubt, but until then . . . let go!' Amethyst yelled.

'What?!' Emerald clung to Amethyst tighter.

'Just let go!'

'I'm not strong enough to fly,' Emerald admitted, forgetting herself entirely.

'I'm not going to let you fall. Loosen your grip and put your arms out. Remember what it's like to be carefree and not planning your next wicked deed. Remember what it was like being a kid. Not having to worry about anything other than simply having fun.'

Emerald didn't move for a few moments, but then, slowly, she loosened the hold she had on her sister's waist and began to lift her arms, until they were stretched out on either side of her like wings. She could feel the rush of the wind between her fingers, the way it tugged at her arms slightly. She took in a deep breath of autumn air that was so cold it made her lungs ache. She felt alive! Even though her cheeks stung from the bite of the chill, she couldn't help but smile, and the tiny bit of light that was buried deep within her began to shine through . . . literally. Emerald's skin was beginning to turn green. She gave off a glow so bright that Amethyst could feel the warmth of it. She turned her head and saw her sister with her arms spread out like a bird, her eyes closed and her teeth bared, not in a wicked snarl but in a childish grin.

'Welcome back, Emerald,' Amethyst whispered, before speeding into another loop-the-loop and then heading back in the direction of the main square.

The children sat bunched together on the grass with their arms round each other, gently weeping. No one had ventured too far from the bandstand. No one wanted to go in search of their parents in case they found them turned to stone, a last look of terror carved on to their faces forever more.

'Best to wait until Amethyst is back. See if something can be done, before we start to panic,' Ivy said solemnly, not wanting to look behind her at her father. Maggie took her hand and sat down with her back to those particular two statues.

'Why don't we practise the song that makes Amethyst concentrate harder so her magic is stronger? That way, when she gets back, we can all help give her strength,' Maggie suggested, but no one wanted to sing. Their hearts were too heavy. 'All right, I'll start. Now, how did it go?' Maggie didn't have a perfect singing voice but she *loved* to sing. In her dad's car, in the bath, on the way to school. It made her happy. If only she could remember the lyrics or how the song went. 'By the golden moon? No, that wasn't it. By the sun, not the moon? Oh, it's no use! I can't remember –'

'*I wish I may . . .*' Eddie sang, and his voice was pitch perfect and crystal clear.

'*I wish I might . . .*' Ivy added.

'*But not on stars I see tonight . . .*' Eddie continued, and now Isaac joined in with Darla, who clapped her hands to the beat of their music.

'*Instead I'll wish upon the moon . . .*' Ivy sang, and Maggie looked at her in shock. 'What? It's catchy!'

'You only heard it once!' Maggie said, giggling.

'I pick things up quickly!' Ivy said.

Eddie, Isaac, Darla and Jennifer then took the main melody and Jamie, Ivy and Maggie took the other bits in between. They sang the song over and over until the other children picked up the words and they were singing it as loudly as they could. Almost without noticing they got to their feet again and stood in a circle, holding hands. It was good to feel just a tiny bit of joy.

'*And hope she hears my hopeful tune!*' Eddie, Isaac, Darla and Jennifer sang brightly.

'*Fiddle di dee and fiddle di doo!*' Maggie, Ivy and Jamie shouted through their laughter.

'*My heart is sweet, my heart is true,*
Fiddle di doo and fiddle di dee,
May the moon shine just for meeeeee!'

They all howled the last note up to the moon as loudly as they could, until a sudden *WHOOSH* cut them off.

'Look! It's Amethyst!' Maggie shouted, and pointed up to the sky. The light of Emerald's glowing skin came into view first and then they saw the sparkling purple magic trailing behind them. Amethyst tipped Emerald off the bristly end of the broom and on to her bottom on the top of the bandstand and then she continued until she landed gently and elegantly on the grass beside the children.

'What happened, Amethyst? Is your sister still wicked?' Maggie cried.

'Oh yes, but I think there's still a chance we can save her.'

'Help me.' Emerald's voice was small and quiet. Just a little sob from the top of the bandstand. 'I can't live another day as a cat or as whatever it is that I am now. Something weird and in between. Something angry and sad and lonely. The curse has taken everything from me.' Emerald's glow was fading and Amethyst knew they only had a few moments before the little sliver of light that was still in her heart, the last tiny shred of the true Emerald, would fade and she would be sucked back into the dark abyss of the demon's curse.

'We have to act fast,' she said.

'We've been practising your song, Amethyst. The one that makes your magic stronger. I think we might have got some of the lyrics wrong, but we're ready to help you in whatever way we can,' Ivy said, grinning.

Amethyst's eyes began to glisten in the moonlight. 'Thank you,' she managed to say through the lump in her throat. 'That really will help, actually.'

Ivy nodded to Eddie, who began to sing and lead everyone else in a much calmer chorus of the song.

'I'm going to need you both,' said Amethyst. 'It'll take every ounce of magic we've got. Emerald's soul is shrouded in darkness and that darkness will want to fight back in order to keep hold of her. So I'm going to need you to promise me one thing.' Amethyst's face was grave and serious. The girls nodded. 'Whatever you happen to see, you can't turn away. Emerald's darkness will do anything it can to stay with her, and it will test you – but we cannot break our stream of magic. We have to see this through until the very end or it won't work. OK?'

'We promise,' Ivy and Maggie said, even though a small shiver ran down both their spines at the thought of what might happen. They glanced at each other and gave a small nod. They could handle it. They knew they could. They'd handled everything up until now extremely well, so how bad could it really be?

'Do it now! Quickly! Before the darkness takes over!' Ivy cried. Emerald's green glow was still only a glimmer and she was clearly straining against whatever evil was working against her.

'OK, girls. Remember what I said. The happiest thought you've got. Channel everything into it. Feel every ounce of hope flowing right down to your fingertips and give her all you've got. Ready?' Amethyst said, holding her arms out.

Maggie and Ivy positioned themselves either side of Amethyst, Ivy on the left, Maggie on the right. They nodded. 'We're ready.'

'Three . . .' said Maggie.

'Two . . .' said Ivy. They raised their hands up to Emerald, who had now got herself to a standing position on the roof of the bandstand.

'One! NOW!' said Amethyst, and together they blasted six streams of beautiful deep-purple magic right into Emerald's heart.

At first Emerald didn't make a sound. Then she let out a scream so horrifying the children behind them stopped mid-song and clutched their ears.

22

The Prophecy is Fulfilled

'KEEP . . . SINGING . . .' Amethyst cried. The children kept
singing and thinking happy, hopeful thoughts, huddling closer
together in order to hear each other. The magic streaming
from Maggie, Ivy and Amethyst's hands grew brighter and
brighter until it hurt their eyes to keep looking at it.

Emerald began to claw like a wild animal at the place where
the magic was entering her heart, swinging her head this way
and that way and howling like a maimed wolf. Suddenly
black magic began to seep out of her skin. It looked like
ink in water as it silently poured out of her, slowly at first,
like little drops of black liquid in a pond, and then all at

once like a tsunami in an ocean. It swirled around her, creating a globe of darkness that whirled and splashed.

'Maggie? Maggie who?' said a voice.

'Dad? DAD!' Maggie looked over her shoulder, but the statue of her father remained. She was certain that it was his voice.

'I don't know anyone called Maggie. And I most certainly do not have a *daughter*.' It *was* Max's voice, loud and clear. There was a gap in the inky black tornado of water, and Maggie could see Emerald's eyes were closed but her lips were moving – the voice was coming from her. The flow of water slowed and streams snaked out and started to form shapes of their own. One whirled upwards and began to take the form of a person. There was a head, then shoulders, and then, suddenly, there was a grown man. When the water formed a face, it was unmistakably Maggie's father.

It opened its mouth and Max's voice came out. 'I live alone with my dog, Frankenstein. Children make too much mess.' The watery version of Maggie's father sank back into the whirlpool around Emerald and was gone. Maggie sobbed silently but still kept her streams of magic strong and pointed directly at Emerald.

'Good girl, Maggie. It's not real. You know how much your father loves you. None of this is real. It's only the darkness doing everything in its power to stay,' Amethyst said soothingly.

'I remember Maggie – she was the daughter I never had. But I have no idea who Ivy is,' said another voice, which sounded like Bill.

'No . . .' Ivy whispered, and she closed her eyes, the colour of her magic suddenly fading.

'Ivy, you must keep your eyes open. Your magic has to be as strong as it possibly can be for this spell to work. I know it's hard and awful, but it'll be over soon. Remember that none of it is real. Not one word,' Amethyst begged, and Ivy slowly opened her eyes a little, squinting through her glasses.

'Whoever this Ivy is, she sounds like a proper little know-it-all. Who would want to spend any time with someone like that?' Ivy's father materialized in front of them in the water. Bill Eerie sipped a cup of tea and looked down his nose at Amethyst, as if Ivy didn't exist. 'How could I ever love someone who was such a know-it-all? No, if only I had a daughter like Maggie.' Bill turned to Maggie and looked at her lovingly. 'Someone brave and bright and strong and courageous. Not a cowardly little clever-clogs who always has her nose in a book. No one like that could ever be *my* daughter. No one like that could ever be *my* daughter . . . No one like that could ever be *my* daughter.' The image of Ivy's father melted back into the watery globe and vanished.

Ivy sniffed hard but did not give in. She concentrated her sadness into hope that they could bring her father back.

'Brace yourselves, girls. This next one might be quite the storm,' Amethyst cried. The black cloud above the mountain began to move swiftly towards them. It loomed nearer and nearer until it was directly overhead. Green lightning crackled threateningly. The water around Emerald parted and whooshed upwards into the cloud, and suddenly it began to rain down upon them in giant black, inky globs. The chorus of children began to shiver as they sang, but they didn't falter. Instead, they gripped each other's hands even more tightly. Emerald stepped forward in her black dress, her eyes darker than ever before despite the steady stream of purple magic still flowing directly into her heart. The wickedness in her knew it might only have moments before it was banished entirely, and it was going to put up a fight.

'*AHHHHHHH!*' Darla began to scream. The drops of inky rain had slowly built a watery version of her mother. It ripped Mrs Unicorn out of her arms and tugged at its head until it came clean off, with an explosion of stuffing that floated down around Darla. 'Mrs Unicorn!' Darla started to sob.

'Keep singing, Darla. Keep singing for Mrs Unicorn,' Isaac coaxed in gentle, soothing tones. 'We can fix her when this is over.'

Darla sucked in a deep breath and suddenly let out her singing voice as loudly as she could. 'I WISH I MAY I WISH I MIGHT!' she shouted, while giving the evil ink-stained version of her mother the hardest stare possible. One by one, every child's parents appeared before them, made out of ink and rain.

'I never loved you,' said Jamie's father.

'Why are you so boring? I don't know how to talk to you,' said Jennifer's mother, as she snatched up her handmade broom from the ground and snapped it in two.

'I've always thought you were so odd,' said Isaac's father, taking Isaac's beloved jar of pond slime from the grass and throwing it to the ground, where it smashed at his feet.

'You're not as clever as you think you are,' said Eddie's father.

These were the worst things the children imagined their parents could say to them. The wickedness in Emerald's heart was destroying any hope the children had left. But there is one thing about evil and darkness: it has no idea just how strong hope can be when you hold on to it tightly enough. So the children held on tighter and tighter and their hope grew stronger and stronger, and they fed off each other's hope too, and sang louder and louder through their tears, until each watery version of their parents went crashing down to the ground with a splash.

'I left because I couldn't stand *you*,' Emerald said to Amethyst in her own voice. 'Because you were and always will be a thorn in my side. How could I ever love a sister who is half the witch I am? A kitchen witch. *Mary Poppins*. Silly little spells. You were holding me back and you know it. That's why you let me go. Why you never came after me. Because you know your magic is so weak and temperamental you might as well be *human*,' Emerald snarled, her eyes so glassy and black that Maggie and Ivy could see themselves and their bright magic reflected in them.

Amethyst closed her eyes.

'No, Amethyst!' Maggie begged. 'Open your eyes! We believe in you!'

But Amethyst suddenly looked defeated.

'Ivy, it's not working! Emerald looks as strong and as evil as ever!' Maggie kept her hands pointed towards Emerald, but she leaned backwards behind Amethyst to talk to Ivy.

'Ivy, didn't Amethyst say something about how everyone is born with a little bit of magic inside them?'

'Yeah . . . so . . .?' Ivy asked, but when Maggie glanced behind them at their friends, all still singing as loudly as they could, Ivy understood. 'Everyone!' she called. 'Keep singing and keep holding hands, but someone take hold of Maggie's right shoulder and someone else take hold of my left so we're one big circle facing Emerald.'

Eddie took hold of Ivy's shoulder but kept hold of Jamie with his free hand. Jennifer did the same on Maggie's side.

'Good! Now, think the happiest and most hopeful thought you possibly can,' Ivy ordered.

Isaac thought about becoming a limnologist: someone who studies ponds and lakes and rivers.

Eddie thought about becoming a teacher and sharing all the exciting things he'd learned.

Jennifer imagined owning a shop filled with the wonderful things she'd made with her own two hands.

Jamie saw himself being on stage in front of thousands of people as a professional dancer.

Darla imagined a room filled from floor to ceiling with Mrs Unicorn's little unicorn babies.

And all the other children thought of the wonderful and amazing things the future would hold. How they would make the most of those years the Crowood Witch wanted to steal. How they would never waste a single second because those seconds belonged to them and no one else. One by one they added their own hopes and dreams and magic to Amethyst's, Maggie's and Ivy's spell to rid Emerald of her darkness.

'We can do this, Amethyst. Everyone believes in you,' Maggie urged.

'Open your eyes and let's finish this.' Ivy gently bumped Amethyst's shoulder, but Amethyst stayed completely still, as Emerald's evil sneer got more and more devious.

Then suddenly Amethyst's eyes shot open and they were glowing the brightest purple any of them had ever seen. Maggie and Ivy could feel not only their own magic pulsing through their veins but also everyone else's own personal style of magic. Each little piece felt strange and different, not like Amethyst's magic at all. They'd become accustomed to that strong, potent magic that allowed Maggie to fly and Ivy to read minds. It was powerful and came with the taste of plums in their mouths and the smell of sugar. The other children's magic was different and had its own power. It felt like a warm hug from your best friend. It smelled like the first day of the summer holidays. It tasted like hot chocolate and toast. It was comfort and happiness. Adventure and hope. It felt familiar and exciting all at once. It was only a little bit of extra magic from each of their friends, but together it made a huge difference, like lots of tiny sparks joining to become a roaring fire.

Now the purple magic streaming out from their fingertips was brighter than ever before. The air filled with the scent of plums, caramel and the earthy smell like after it has rained.

Emerald started to step backwards as it got stronger, and suddenly she began to scream again. 'STOP! STOP! PLEASE!' she yelled, but the sound of her voice began to get deeper and demonic. It no longer sounded like Emerald any more. Because it *wasn't* Emerald. It was the wickedness in her heart separating from Emerald's soul. It was the curse lifting.

'IT'S WORKING!' Ivy cried over the children's singing, and the good news spurred them on. Their hope rushed through their hands, right the way through to Maggie's, Ivy's and Amethyst's fingertips, and straight into Emerald's heart. The black in Emerald's eyes began to shrink away, revealing the white in her eyes and the green they used to be when she was a child, full of a zest for life and adventure. The black in Emerald's dress started to disappear, starting from the hem, slowly at first and then in a rush all the way up to her shoulders, to reveal the colour her dress must have once been: a lush and vibrant green. The feline claws in her feet retracted and she was once again left with her soft witch's feet (which looked very much like human feet except her toes came together in the middle to create a point – which is why witches always wear pointy shoes, of course). And Emerald's damp and lank hair suddenly became curly and lusciously green. She *was* an earth witch, after all.

All the darkness whooshed out of Emerald and into the sky. It dispersed into the black cloud above, which crackled violently, threatening to unleash every bolt of lightning it had. The children kept singing, but their voices began to wobble as they cast their eyes up to the smoke, which they were certain would sizzle them to a crisp. But Emerald had other plans. A bolt of pure and bright green lightning shot up from her hand into the sky. It was so powerful it sent a shock wave across the square, knocking Maggie, Ivy, Amethyst and the circle of children on to their backs, and breaking the purple stream of magic, which was of no more use.

The spell had worked. All the darkness was out of Emerald's heart. She was rid of the evil that had consumed her for three hundred years, but now it was above them, mixing with Emerald's spell. The smoke billowed and swirled and rocketed through the air with the sound of a thousand jet engines. A face appeared and roared with anger. Both Amethyst and Emerald gasped, and quickly their hands found each other.

'She's been in your head this whole time?' Amethyst asked, her voice shaking.

'Not her. Only the curse,' Emerald said. Maggie and Ivy shared a look, understanding that the face they had just seen was the original Crowood Witch.

'There's so much of it . . .' Amethyst said, choking back a sob. 'Sister, there's so much sadness and rage and wickedness up there.'

'I know.' Emerald couldn't bring herself to look upwards. She knew what was there. 'We need to destroy it, or it'll wreak havoc on the Earth before the night is out.'

'We'll follow your lead.' Amethyst took up a position behind her sister, but Emerald put her hands on her shoulders.

'No, sister. I need *you*. I'm out of practice when it comes to hope and happiness.'

'And I need your knowledge of the darkness and exactly what it is we're facing. I'm not strong enough to defeat it, and yet you lived with it every day for three hundred years without being entirely consumed by it.' Amethyst looked into Emerald's newly green eyes; eyes she remembered from her childhood, which glistened with tears and something her sister hadn't felt in a long time. Hope.

'Together?' Emerald smiled and held out her hand.

'Together.' Amethyst intertwined her fingers with her sister's and together they turned to confront the evil face in the smoke cloud. It had formed a mouth and began to cackle in a deep and menacing tone that rattled the windows of the buildings around the square. 'And we need all of you too,' she added to the group of children.

'We're with you,' said Maggie, taking hold of Amethyst's shoulder.

'Every step of the way,' said Ivy, nervously placing her hand on Emerald's shoulder.

'I promise I don't bite,' Emerald said softly. 'Not any more, at least.'

One by one the children clambered back on to their feet and lined up beside Maggie and Ivy, joining hands again so that they became one long united line.

'*I wish I may, I wish I might,*' Emerald began to sing, and Amethyst let out a laugh so loud it rivalled the sound of the cackling smoke. Between then, Amethyst, Emerald, Maggie, Ivy and every other child began to think their happiest and most hopeful thoughts. Thoughts of what their lives could be like one day. Of what the *world* could be like one day.

There was laughter, adventure, long summers, cosy winters, parents, guardians, siblings, family, friends and love . . . so much love. More love than any of them could contain in their bodies. It spilled out of them, wave upon wave. It travelled through their hearts, through their joined hands, and all the way along to Amethyst and Emerald, who were now so filled up with sisterly love they both thought they might burst.

They let the love and hope and happiness fly out of them in a great stream of purple and green magic – not from their hands this time, but straight from their hearts. It twisted its way through the square and up into the mouth of the giant face in the smoke cloud. The magic was so bright and so powerful that it filled the black smoke with huge green and purple fireworks that burst in vibrant showers of sparkles.

Maggie and Ivy thought they heard the face scream 'NOOOOOOOO!' But Emerald and Amethyst's firework display drowned out the sound. It only took moments for the smoke to dissolve into nothingness and to leave a clear and starry night sky behind, where the blue moon looked down on them proudly. They had rid Emerald of her darkness, and rid the world of it too.

After three hundred years, the prophecy of the Crowood Witch was finally fulfilled.

23
Time To Go Home

'It's over!' Amethyst announced as pink and green sparks rained down around them. 'The Crowood Witch has been defeated!'

'But I thought *she* was the Crowood Witch?' said Darla, hiding behind Amethyst's legs, not wanting to take her eyes off Emerald in case she put a spell on her when her back was turned.

'I *was*, but only because I let the darkness consume me.' Emerald crouched so that she and Darla were eye to eye. 'I wasn't born evil. I just let evil take the reins for a while, but I'm back to my old self now. Thanks to you.' Emerald picked up the body of Mrs Unicorn, which was lying in the damp grass. Then she waved her hand and Mrs Unicorn's head floated over, a little muddy. Emerald gave her fingers a flourish and the unicorn began to glow green for a moment where the seams had been torn. When the light faded, Mrs Unicorn was restored as good as new. Darla, forgetting her fear of Emerald, ran to her, snatched the stuffed toy from her grasp and hugged it close while kissing it over and over again.

'Your hair!' Ivy reached out and touched the ends of Maggie's raven-black hair.

'*Your* hair!' Maggie picked up the ends of Ivy's blonde plaits and gave them a wiggle. All traces of Amethyst's magic were gone. Maggie and Ivy giggled and fell into a hug, both holding each other as tightly as they could.

'Hang on,' said Eddie. 'How do we know you won't give in to evil again?'

'How do we know that any of us won't?' Amethyst said. 'We're all capable of both good and evil, and we're all equally capable of letting one win over the other.'

Eddie nodded and gave Emerald a small half-smile.

'How did you survive all this time with that . . . that –' Amethyst pointed up to the sky where the smoke and that evil face used to be – 'inside your heart and your head? It must have been awful.'

'Because, Amethyst, when you tied us together with the spell that kept me as a cat in that house, you tied a little piece of yourself to me. That amethyst that hung round my neck on a cat collar for three centuries was a sliver of you and the goodness that's in your heart and the hope you had that one day we'd be reunited as *us*. The real us. You believed that there was still some good in me, and you used some of your own goodness to keep that part of me alive. To ensure it wouldn't be completely overcome by darkness. Your kindness is your strongest magic. It's stronger than I ever gave you credit for. I'm sorry, Amethyst. I'm so sorry.' Emerald took her sister's hand and raised it to her lips, where she kissed it and then held it to her cheek.

'So, it's over? None of us have to worry about our hearts being eaten any more?' Maggie asked.

Emerald laughed, but it wasn't a cackle. In fact, it didn't sound evil at all. It sounded like Amethyst's laugh. Like a wind chime caught in a breeze. 'It's over,' Emerald said. 'And I'm very glad I never had to eat anyone's heart. I bet they taste *dreadful*.'

'Ivy, did you hear that? Ivy? . . . Where's Ivy?' Maggie looked around wildly for her best friend, who had suddenly disappeared. Her heart began to pound in her chest, thinking the worst, until she spotted Ivy by the statues of their fathers, looking up at them mournfully. Maggie ran to her and the others followed. For a moment, they'd forgotten. They'd been so pleased that the Crowood Witch had been defeated, and that they were safe once more, that they'd forgotten about the silent statues surrounding them.

'There must be something you can do!' Ivy let her tears fall freely down her face, unable to contain her sadness. Emerald knelt by Ivy's side, her knees in the wet grass, beckoned Maggie over to her too, and she took them both by the shoulders.

'There isn't anything *I* can do,' Emerald said, but before they began to panic, she added, 'but there is something *you* can do.'

'What?' Ivy took the ends of her plaits and twirled them between her fingers. 'We don't have any magic any more.'

'Ivy, don't tell me you've forgotten already?' Amethyst took one of Ivy's hands and squeezed it.

'Everyone has a little bit of magic,' Maggie said, wiping her tears on her sleeves, realizing what Amethyst meant. 'That's how we defeated that darkness together. It wasn't only Amethyst and Emerald's magic; it was all our magic coming together.'

'But I don't know what my magic is or how to use it.'

'Trust your instincts.' Emerald let go of them both.

Maggie stood in front of her father. She looked up at his stony face and noticed how Max didn't look anything like himself. He looked scared and confused. Her father was always so carefree and sure of himself, and she missed him so much. Maggie felt an ache in her chest, and she closed her eyes and held on to that ache. It was so painful. It felt like a knot in her heart that was filled with sadness and grief and sorrow and the thought of the days ahead she'd have to live without her father. How empty they'd be without his laughter and silliness. Without his wonderful home-cooked meals and his failed attempts at breakfast. Without his creativity and his hare-brained ideas. Without his kindness and warmth. Maggie leaned into that pain and thought of Max's face when she'd read him one of her stories and how proud he had been. She closed her eyes.

Ivy looked up at her own father. A man usually so clever he could think his way out of any situation, but this time the Crowood Witch had bested him. The look of terror carved on to Bill's stony features was almost too much for Ivy to bear. All those horrible things the Crowood Witch had made the watery version of him say weren't true and she knew it. Her father was kind and loving. He always made her feel cherished and cared-for, and she knew he was proud to have her as a daughter. He loved Maggie like a daughter too, but Ivy knew that didn't mean there was less space for her. She knew that was the wonderful thing about love. Love didn't stay the same size, to be divided up between people. That would mean the more people there were, the less love everyone got. Like a cake being shared between hundreds, where everyone would only get a tiny mouthful. No. Love expanded. Love simply grew and got bigger and encompassed anyone and everyone who needed it. You could take as much love as you needed and there would still be enough to go around. She knew that, anatomically, hearts are only a little bigger than the size of your fist, but she also knew that her father's heart was the biggest she'd ever known. Ivy thought of the pride on her father's face whenever she solved a tricky equation or told him a fact he didn't already know, and she closed her eyes.

An almighty *CRACK!* filled the air, and Maggie and Ivy jumped back from the statues.

'LOOK!' Maggie pointed up at the statues' outstretched hands and saw that the stone was beginning to crumble away. Underneath were Max and Bill's human hands, wriggling to try to get free.

'Help us!' Ivy said as she clambered to her feet and ran to the statue of her father. All the children ran to their aid and began pulling chunks of stone away until Max and Bill were free and, more importantly, *alive*.

'Maggie? Maggie! Oh, my Maggie!' Max wrapped his arms round his daughter and kissed the top of her head over and over and over again until Maggie pulled away so that she could look into his face. She put her hands on his cheeks and stared deep into his eyes.

'You remember me?'

'Of *course* I remember you. How could I not? You're my favourite person in the whole wide world!' Max picked up his daughter and swung her round and round until they fell down on to the grass, giggling.

'Ivy! Is that you? Where are my glasses?' Bill stumbled forward, reaching out ahead of him to steady his footsteps. Ivy found his glasses lying in the grass but still intact, and pressed them into his hands. Once they were firmly on the bridge of his nose, his eyes lit up and a smile spread across his face from ear to ear. 'Oh, Ivy! It's so wonderful to see you. I was having the worst ever nightmare about losing you.'

'Really?' Ivy sniffled. 'The worst ever?'

'What on earth do you mean, "*really*"? Of course it was. Out of all my projects, experiments and inventions, you are without a doubt the greatest. The one thing in my life that I am most proud of will always be you, Ivy.' Ivy couldn't speak, so she threw her arms round her father and held him as tightly as she could.

'Come on, everyone!' Isaac clapped his hands together. 'We've got a job to do!' The children ran to find the statues of their parents to give them a little bit of love and bring them back to life. To bring them home.

'So the prophecy came true! *When the thirteenth moon is blue, two sisters, fierce and brave and true, will send the witch to death's embrace, and to her final resting place.* You were the two sisters!' Ivy cheered.

'Oh, I don't think we were,' said Amethyst.

'No, me neither,' said Emerald, with a wide grin.

'What do you mean?' asked Maggie.

'You were the two who broke the circle. You were the two who brought Emerald back, and without you we never would have been able to defeat the darkness,' Amethyst explained.

'The prophecy wasn't talking about me and Amethyst. It was talking about you two. The Double Trouble Society,' Emerald said.

'But . . . we aren't sisters,' Ivy said.

Amethyst scoffed immediately. 'Of course you are. You and your fathers don't share any blood, but would you ever doubt that you're family?'

Ivy and Maggie shook their heads, their eyes round and hopeful.

'Exactly. You're sisters because you feel it in here.' Amethyst tapped the place on her chest where her heart was beating beneath the skin.

'She's right, Ivy.' Maggie smiled. 'You've always been my sister.'

'And you've always been mine.' Ivy snaked her arm through Maggie's and squeezed it tightly. Emerald did the same to Amethyst.

'So . . . who are you, exactly?' asked Bill, adjusting his glasses.

'OK, Dad,' Ivy said. 'Don't freak out, but . . . this is Emerald. She is – well, was – the Crowood Witch. But she's not any more!'

'The . . . Crowood Witch?' Max said, his mouth hanging open.

'And this is her sister, Amethyst,' Maggie said. Bill and Max exchanged a concerned look but smiled politely at the sisters all the same. 'They helped us defeat the curse that created the Crowood Witch. They're the reason we're all safe and will be forever!'

'Sorry about earlier,' Emerald said sheepishly. 'Wasn't quite myself.'

'Are you ready for us to go home?' Amethyst twirled her hand and the two halves of Jennifer's broom floated towards her, then they attached themselves back together with a soft purple glow and the broom gently landed in Amethyst's hand.

'Home? Where's home?' Emerald asked.

Amethyst smiled. 'Anywhere we can be together.'

'You mean . . . you're leaving?' Maggie asked.

'We can't stay here,' Amethyst said softly.

'Why not?' Ivy said, disappointed.

'Because I've been the Crowood Witch,' Emerald said sadly.

'No, you *used* to be,' Maggie said.

'I don't think people forget that easily.' Emerald cast her eyes downwards.

'There are ways to fix that . . .' Amethyst raised her glowing purple fingers, but Emerald quickly snatched her hand away and extinguished the light.

'No . . . no more of that kind of magic. If I'm going to live somewhere, I want to do it honestly. No more darkness, no more forgetting . . . just happy, kind, good magic from now on,' Emerald pleaded. Amethyst nodded.

'The people of Crowood Peak might not forget, but we do forgive,' said Max, holding out his hand. Emerald tentatively placed her hand in his and let him shake it firmly, without hesitation.

'It's true. We're a village that believes in second chances. Goodness knows we all need them from time to time,' Bill said, following Max's lead and shaking Emerald's hand.

'Could be kind of perfect,' Amethyst said with a smile. 'I mean, we've already got a house here. It might need some redecorating again, but . . . it's home.'

Emerald looked around at their kind and open faces and felt something squeeze her heart, and for the first time in a long while, it wasn't something dark or sinister. Instead, it felt warm and loving.

'Well, after three hundred years spent in one place, I would probably be incredibly homesick if I ever left,' she murmured.

'Then don't leave,' Ivy said, as she took one of Emerald's hands and led her in the direction of Hokum House.

'And if anyone has anything to say about it, well – that's what friends are for,' Maggie said, as she took Emerald's other hand and skipped along in front of her.

'Friends?' Emerald gasped softly.

'Yes. Friends,' Ivy said.

'And family,' Amethyst said, gently floating ahead of them on the broom. 'Come on, sister. Race you home?'

'Last one there is a mangy feline!' Emerald shouted, and with a kick of her bare feet she took off from the ground and zoomed ahead of Amethyst, who immediately followed on her broom. The sound of their tinkling laughter filled the air and Maggie and Ivy ran after them down the road, but they were no match for the speed of the two witch sisters. Their purple and green glittering magic trailed across the sky, and then their silhouettes dashed across the brilliant blue moon.

'The Double Trouble Society strikes again!' Maggie gave Ivy a high five and then jumped as high as she could, both her fists raised in triumph in the air.

'Well, Maggie. Turns out you were right,' Ivy said.

'I'm always right!' Maggie laughed with her chest puffed out. 'Wait a minute . . . Right about what?'

Ivy laughed and linked arms with her best friend in the whole entire world, and said:

'That really was our best adventure yet.'

Epilogue

Jemima slowly awoke to find herself on a sofa in a house that wasn't her own. It took her a moment to remember the events that had led up to the headache that now pounded behind her eyes and caused her throat to feel dry and scratchy.

She made her way to the front door and opened it just in time to see two witches land on the front lawn. One was barefoot and dressed in the most dazzling green dress. Her long, black, curly hair looked so soft that Jemima wanted to touch it, and her eyes were so green they looked like real gemstones.

The other witch Jemima already knew as Amethyst, but she looked so different. She seemed to be sparkling in the moonlight, as if her skin was filled with magic. They both turned to look at her as she opened the door.

The witches were quickly joined by Ivy and Maggie, and then suddenly by the whole group of children and their parents too. They stood gazing at Jemima, who had been asleep through the entire night. She coughed before she spoke, the words feeling odd in her throat after not speaking for what felt like an eternity.

'What did I miss?'

THE
DOUBLE TROUBLE
SOCIETY
QUIZ

Thanks for coming to Crowood Peak and joining us on our spooky and magical adventure! Did you enjoy it? Now it's time to find out whether you were paying attention to the story. Can you answer all the questions below correctly?

Love from Ivy and Maggie

(The Double Trouble Society)

xxx

1 What colour are Amethyst's eyes?
a Purple
b Black
c Midnight blue

2 Ivy and Maggie share the same birthday. But what date is it?
a Friday 13th
b October 31st
c February 29th

3 What does Isaac take to school in a jar every day?
a Fish bait
b Slime
c Frogspawn

4 What is the name of the cat who lives at Hokum House?
a Codswallop
b Ramshackle
c Tumbledown

5 What colour was the moon on the night of the Festival for the Twelve?
a Maroon
b Blue
c Silver

6 What nickname does Maggie's dad have for her?
a Pumpkin
b Marshmallow
c Candyfloss

7 What is the name of Crowood Peak's librarian?
a Mrs Grumpy
b Mrs Moody
c Mrs Disgruntled

8 What are Maggie's and Ivy's favourite flavours of cupcake?
a Chocolate and caramel
b Bubblegum and popcorn
c Strawberries and cream

9 What is Ivy's middle name?
a Willow
b Maple
c Holly

10 What does Maggie want to be when she grows up?
a A deep-sea diver
b An accountant
c A writer

11 What is the name of the school caretaker?
a Mr Broom
b Mr Woodman
c Mr Ogre

IF YOU SCORED . . .

8–11 WOW! With a score like that, we're making you an honorary member of The Double Trouble Society. Congratulations!

5–7 Hmm — a good effort, but it looks like you might need to brush up on your magical knowledge. We recommend starting with *Magic for the Tragic* or *Craft for the Daft*.

0–4 It's clear that the Crowood Witch has put a charm on your memory, and you've forgotten the entire story! You'll have to go back to the beginning and read it all over again!

ALSO BY
CARRIE HOPE FLETCHER

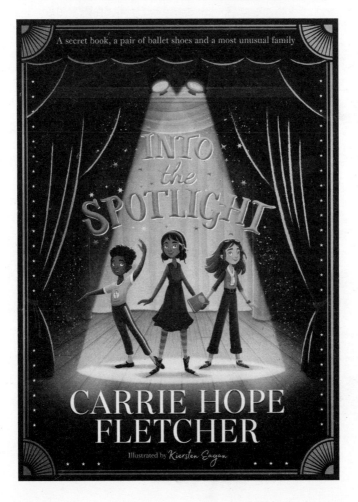

A secret book, a pair of ballet shoes and a most unusual family

INTO *the* SPOTLIGHT

CARRIE HOPE FLETCHER

Illustrated by *Kiersten Eagan*